What they are saying abo

"Navigating the gamut of human relationships is never easy, particularly in the South, where the undercurrent of racism simmers below the surface, but Billy Beasley has written a suspenseful story that keeps you enthralled and doesn't let go until the very last page."

—Kathryn Gauci, USA TODAY Bestselling Author

"Beasley's characters are as natural, intriguing, and as full of life as the Carolina coast they call home. Their conflicts play out in a low country Eden that is as stirring and primal as the passions of its people."

—Joseph McSpadden, Host of the Village Night Owl Podcast and Contributing Editor, *Okra* Magazine.

MELTDOWN

Also by Billy Beasley:

The River Hideaway

The Preacher's Letter

The Girl in the River

Home

MELTDOWN

A Novel

Billy Beasley

REDHAWK
PUBLICATIONS

MELTDOWN

ISBN: 978-1-959346-54-8 (Paperback)

Library of Congress Control Number: 2024938465

Any references to historical events, real people, or real places are used fictitiously. Names, characters, and places are products of the author's imagination.

Front Cover: Photograph by Billy Beasley

Book design: Robert T Canipe

Printed in the United States of America.

First printing edition 2024.

Redhawk Publications
The Catawba Valley Community College Press
2550 Hwy 70 SE
Hickory NC 28602

https://redhawkpublications.com

For my son, Micah Brooks Beasley.

Billie Jo,
Hope you enjoy
Micah 6:8
Billy Beasley

ACKNOWLEDGMENTS:

My wife, Julie. Thank you for your love, support, encouragement and for being my first reader.

Patty, and the team at Redhawk Publications. Thank you for the opportunity.

PROLOGUE

Saturday (11:45 PM)

"I am fixing to blow your brains out."

The owner of this eloquent, cleverly articulated statement is standing over me with a pistol pointed directly at my chest. That's good. I would not want him to shoot me in the face. It would be such an abuse of my natural good looks.

It was just the type of remark I expected from him, though this is the first time I have enjoyed the pleasure of his company. Chalk it up to my high degree of intuition but I would wager that any statement containing a word with more than two syllables would probably be a stretch for his vocabulary. And his use of the word fixing produced an inner smile to a child raised on the fringes of the Deep South.

He reeked of nicotine and alcohol. There was a gaudy NASCAR cap perched on his head with a severely cupped bill and possibly eight different colors. He was a skinny man with big dark eyes that reminded me of something out of a horror movie. I am no aficionado of horror movies. I don't watch them because much like the image of his face—I fear that they may keep me awake at night. His face was so narrow that it reminded me of a chicken. Splotches of wiry hair sprouted on his chin perhaps in an attempt to enhance his masculine image.

The oversized beak that dominated his face reinforced my part chicken part man analogy. Why shoot me and waste a bullet? Hell, he could just peck me to death.

The hand that gripped the pistol tightly shook like a worn alcoholic reaching for the first drink of the day. I debated as to the type of firearm that was pointed in my direction. Possibly a thirty-eight, though I confess that my knowledge of guns is quite limited. From a distance of less than eight feet it really doesn't matter. I am in quite the predicament. I guess I can't blame him for being upset. I glanced at his wife who was beside me in their bed. She has not moved or spoken. I can hear her breathing faintly. She was sitting up—using the sheet to cover her unclothed body.

"Don't you look at her again you son-of-a-bitch," he said slowly—with heavy emphasis on the bitch part.

I had underestimated his language skills. He had spoken a four-syllable word with clarity—skipping from a two-syllable word straight to a word containing four syllables. I could barely contain my exhilaration. It reminded me for some peculiar reason of the kid in *A Christmas Story*, who while trying to get the other kid to stick his tongue on the flagpole, skipped the traditional steps and went for the triple dog dare. People like routines and a sense of civility. I debated as to whether I should point this out to him, but the look on his face, and also the gun in his trembling hand, led me to believe that given his current state of mind he might not appreciate my linking life to a movie or a television show as I so often am apt to do. Besides, now I am questioning whether it is four syllables or four separate words. I may have unduly granted him too much credit. This disappointed me greatly. Perhaps I will have the opportunity to research this matter at a later time.

Considering the lull in the conversation I decided that it was time for me to add some depth to a dialogue that so far has been woefully lacking with intellect. "If you insist on shooting me—I would prefer that you do so while I am standing up. I wouldn't want you to miss me and hit your wife." I lightly touched her quivering thigh under the covers as I moved slowly out of the bed.

By injecting myself into the conversation I appear to have confused him. "Uh, no, uh," he stammered.

I continued to rise from the bed as he searched for a suitable one-syllable word. I picked my dark blue boxers off the floor and slipped them on smoothly. Cowboys are supposed to want to die with their boots on. I don't own a pair of boots, but I sure do not care to be naked if he shoots me. I walked to the other side of the room so that the gun is no longer aimed in the vicinity of his wife. Ah chivalry, that is me.

"You stop right there."

He had found his comfort zone. All one-syllable words and delivered with such precision. They were quite effective unless you considered the fact that I had already ceased moving before he uttered a sound.

"What's your name?" his voice quavered in harmony with the quaking gun in his hand.

"Billy Langdon," I answered slowly in hopes that he could understand. I thought it best not to confuse him and I don't think it would take much under the best of circumstances, which this is surely not.

"Billy," he replied with a smirk. "What kind of name is that?"

I smiled broadly. "Starts with a B, ends with a y, with ill in the middle."

He held the gun out straighter. It helped steady his hand momentarily.

"Real wise ass, aren't you?"

I assumed that was a rhetorical question and in no need of a response, even from someone with my bountiful wit.

"Well Bill, you are going to die tonight."

Why do people do that to my name? What is so complicated about saying, Billy? People ask me my name and then immediately shorten it. I have even had my name reduced in email messages. One letter. No one is that busy. I wonder what person decided long ago that at a certain age Billy must be shortened to Bill. My dad's name was Bill. It has never been my name.

Polite people often ask which I prefer and I always state, Billy. Of course, many of our northern friends, who have moved to our region in droves and often assume because we speak slower, we must be challenged mentally will remark, "Oh, Billy Bob." Now each scholarly giant that comes up with this crafty line assumes that they were the first person to think of it. There is nothing quite as annoying as someone who thinks they are funnier, or smarter, or both than they genuinely are. But when you consider an idiot like the guy in front of me—I can understand why some of us get a bad rap.

I speculated whether or not people had met Billy Graham and immediately shortened his name to suit their comfort level. One thing we can safely ascertain is that Billy Graham would never have been in my current quandary. I began to contemplate as my overactive mind is prone to do about other men that kept the name Billy. Billy the Kid, who if half the stories about him are true, probably shot anyone who referred to him as Bill. Billy Joel, who I am sure no one ever referred to as Bill Joel. There is no flow to Bill Joel, and after all, he is a gifted musician.

The gun wobbled in a different manner and I determined that it would probably be best to return to more important matters than famous people named Billy. Maybe I could get back to it later if I am lucky, really lucky.

Oddly, despite my current dilemma, I felt a calmness that bordered on being eerie. It is late Saturday night, and this has easily proven to be the strangest week of my life. It all began the previous Sunday afternoon, but I think the signs were well in place before that.

This past winter I must have driven behind over one hundred cars that had one brake light out. Surely it must have been a sign. Maybe it was from God. Could it be that he was winking at me with what was coming in the spring? I even drove behind one car that had one brake light out and the other one was covered in water. The bulb shone dimly through the water and when the lady drove off, the water splashed from side to side. Even someone with my highly advanced perception skills can't decipher the meaning of that. If it was God sending a message, why couldn't he just talk like the rest of us? God's plan can be a bit confusing, regardless of what they tell you in church on Sunday morning. That is unless you believe those people that say God talks to them all day long. Many years ago, a preacher informed me that God told him what type of motor oil to buy for his car. I can't recall the brand. Surely, considering the era, it could not have been something other than Pennzoil. I mean not even God would possess the audacity to challenge Arnold Palmer—the spokesperson for Pennzoil in those days, would he?

Another thought emerged that saddened and comforted me all at the same time. My mom, a wonderfully spiritual woman, who prayed for me without ceasing, will not be wounded if this current scenario resulted with the end of my life. Two years ago, my three older sisters and I had to put her in a home when her dementia required around the clock care.

Remarkably, she knows who I am when I visit, but that is about the extent of her memory.

The woman who always had such great faith and God allowed her to be reduced to a shell of what she once was. I have placed myself in a position where I deserved my fate, but my kind, gentle, sweet mother did nothing to warrant such a horrific disease. I guess that I am a little, make that a lot, peeved with God for allowing my mom to fall into the blackened shadows of dementia. But that is not the only matter that I have been irate with him about.

There was a time when my life was not so darkened. I was married and we were happy or so it seemed. We belonged to a nice church near our modest house. I even served as a deacon. Kind of ironic, don't you think? From a deacon to the moment at hand. I can see my obituary now. Former deacon, Billy Langdon, met his demise Saturday night when the husband of the woman he was sleeping with returned unexpectedly and shot him.

We were married for five years when she became pregnant but on the day that the baby was born—my life unraveled. I am a white southerner, as my ex-wife is. The baby arrived into this world a few shades darker than either of us. Imagine my shock to witness the birth of what I thought was my son only to realize my sneaking suspicions that the Italian assistant minister was a little too friendly with my wife were not grounded in paranoia.

I walked out of the hospital and never saw or spoke to her again. She and the minister married as soon as the ink on the divorce papers were dry. He was counseling my wife over spiritual matters when it blossomed into afternoon meetings in cheap hotels.

They moved out west and he landed a job in a large church as the lead pastor. I could write a book on that decision by the church but that might bore you and besides, there is a lot of this story I have yet to share with you.

"Hey, I have a gun pointed at you."

The raised voice snaps me back to the present moment. I guess I should be asking God for help but at the moment I don't particularly care about my current dilemma. Life has proven to be one grand disappointment and my fury at him since the day I walked out of the hospital has only escalated over the past two decades.

I thought back to the previous Sunday and the trail that brought me to this house. It was a doozy of a week. Sit back, grab a cool beverage, relax, and I will tell you all about it.

Sunday

The man seated in the next booth cursed loudly once again. "I ordered my damn beer five minutes ago. And there is no telling when my food will get here," he added for emphasis. He looked around at the people seated nearby as if he expected that they would surely understand his unpleasant dilemma. They responded by shying away—avoiding any eye contact. I, on the other hand, chose not to.

The jerk I am staring at is a large man and I am fairly certain that he is only a few years older than me but much worse for the wear. His wife is seated across the table from him. She is a frail woman with hair that is a mixture of gray and white with a bluish tint that you normally see on a woman much older. She stared down at the table and fidgeted with her napkin. There was little doubt in my mind that she had been humiliated by the idiot seated across from her on numerous occasions and probably suffered abuses from his heavy hands. She probably wished for a nearby rock big enough for her to crawl under and hide before he gets worse. And he will get worse. Men like him always do.

Seated with me on the opposite side of the booth is my friend Thomas, and his girlfriend from South Africa, Angela. They arrived at my house on Friday night. Thomas lives in Raleigh, and he brought Angela to the coast for the weekend. His car is in the parking lot, packed, and ready for the return trip home after lunch. We began our meal with their famous seafood chowder, which I often picked up on cold winter days and enjoyed at home. We were finished with the assorted seafood dishes we had ordered, though Angela kept picking at her food occasionally. I loved watching her explore the different things in our country, such as food. Yesterday, we went to the Boardwalk for Britt's donuts. She tasted the sugary delicacy and stated in her pleasing accent, "Delightful, absolutely delightful."

Thomas turned his head partially in the direction of the jerk behind him and smiled. He never seemed to have an uptight moment in his life. He is nearing forty and has never been married. I think he likes it that way, though he talks about wanting marriage and kids. He has enjoyed several long-distance relationships but South Africa is a stretch even for him.

Angela is tall with dark skin, and a firm body that flows in symmetry like the colors in a beautiful painting. And by painting, I mean something that I can actually understand what it is and not a canvas that appeared as if someone lined up across the room and shot paintballs at. She is not striking, not beautiful by any means, but sexiness flows generously from her. Some women try so hard and it will never be for them. It is not something that can be derived from makeup, apparel, or rehearsed motions that make a woman truly sexy. It is something that stems naturally from within. Angela has it to such a degree that each place we have visited women stare at her as well as the men. The difference is that the women turn away with a dismayed look etched upon their faces. They make catty remarks to those around them, especially to other women—mainly because they know that she has something that they never will. It is also why the men continue to stare, even after they have been given the evil look from their wives or girlfriends.

They are drawn to look at her. I know this because I possessed such fascinating insight into people and because I have taken a couple of peeks myself. I am sure it does not concern Thomas that I have observed and appreciated her. In fact, I think he would probably be a tad disappointed if I had not. We men are a shallow bunch when it comes to the pleasure that we derive from having a woman on our arm that garners attention the moment she entered a room.

The waitress gingerly approached the incensed man and placed the frosted mug of beer on the table. "It's about fricking time," he snorted, before gulping heavily from his beer. "And how much longer do I have to wait for my food?" He took a napkin that was too small for the job and wiped the splatter from the remnants of the beer that did not make it into his jumbo-sized mouth. It was hard to believe he could miss something that immense.

The waitress appeared to be in her early thirties. She was cute and had long beautiful blonde hair. There was also unmistakable weariness etched in her face. I have witnessed that same fatigued reflection before. For months now, a face of disenchantment greeted me each morning in the bathroom mirror. She concealed her pain with a little makeup. I disguised mine with cleverly worded observations and an array of dazzling smiles.

Frequently, and especially of late, the more challenging part of the day is waking to the early light of dawn. It should be the best part of the day. The stillness of early morning is fresh, offering new prospects for the day. But I lay there feeling barrenness at what has been lost and what has never been. I know without a doubt that she wrestles with these same thoughts.

Some people get past their struggles by having children and placing nearly all the emphasis on them. Discontented dreams and fears buried within kids. It also is something that children are not born into this world asking for and they would be better off without growing up believing they are the center of the universe. I have been single for a long time and I have dated equal numbers of women that had kids and those that did not. She has no little ones. I don't know why I feel so certain about the matter but trust me. I am correct.

Her eyes closed briefly for a scant few seconds and the forced smile vanishes. Maybe she is having a fantasy about what she would like to be able to do given the present circumstances. Right about now, I would wager that she would like to have his plate of food and then dump it right on his colossal head. Hopefully, in the flight of her imagination, the food is piping hot.

She opened her eyes and forced a smile. "I'm sorry that you have had to wait. Your food will be out shortly."

"Yeah, that is what you said the last fricking time," he bellowed, before draining the remainder of his beer. He tapped his mug three times on the table as he eyed her with a stiffened scowl. She smiled nicely, trying in vain to diffuse the beast in front of her. "I'll do my best to serve your food shortly sir, and I will be right back with another beer."

She turned to leave the table and her eyes fell on me. I smiled and offered a slight twist of my head. She shook her head ever so slightly and closed her eyes tightly once again, before walking away. I bet if I would have offered her my best smile, she would have forgotten all about the moron she was forced to make nice with.

Thomas and Angela were discussing their plans for the coming week and I had nothing to offer to the discussion, so I observed the ill-mannered idiot for the next few minutes. He is one of those unbearable, red-faced, big-bellied men that viewed eating as somewhat of a recreational pursuit. He probably spent a good deal of time searching for just the right buffet. You know the kind where you could eat for days at the economical price of $14.95. He probably finished lunch, belched heartily, and turned his next thought to what he craved for dinner. He is also one of those people that did not know enough to be embarrassed by his insufferable behavior.

He sensed my scrutiny and his eyes moved toward mine and locked in. I looked at him without expression. "What the hell are you looking at?" he barked.

People speak of a defining life altering moment. The crossroad they approach and summon the courage to take the unfamiliar route. That time was present for me and I knew it as certainly as I have ever known anything in the forty-eight years that I have been on this earth. I don't know exactly where to trace what is going to happen next. Perhaps it is tied to the mom I worshipped that now is reduced to gazing vacantly into space struggling to land a solitary thought. Maybe it is my anger at God because each time I leave her she asks me to take her home. I don't think she even means the home that was sold to pay the several grand per month to house her in a facility that depressed me each time I drove into the parking lot. More likely it is the house by the old trolley tracks in Sea Gate that long ago burned to the ground. The one she lived in with her mom, dad, two sisters, and a brother who died early in life.

Maybe it is that I am tired of being a nice guy. Nice guys get stomped on trying to do the right thing. Nice guys don't get the girl they want. Some bastard with a fat wallet wins that battle. Heck, let's get really deep. I was tall, skinny, and frail as a boy and an easy target for bullies. Sometimes I refused to fight and went home cloaked in my shame. I wasn't smart enough to realize the bully was afraid also. Sometimes I think of how I would like to hunt some of those guys down and see if they can take me today. Oh hell, I am no fighter but at 6'4, and a fit 215 pounds, with devilish blue eyes I ain't frail any longer. I know the eyes have nothing to do with my size or ability to fight but I thought I would throw that in for good measure to make sure that you were paying attention.

"I asked what the hell you are looking at?"

I continued to look him in the eye. He stood up, though it was an obvious challenge to work his belly out from under the table and walked over to our booth. Thomas started to speak, but I placed my hand on his arm. "I got this," I stated in a low unconcerned voice.

He stood there trying to intimidate me. He wore Wrangler jeans and a bright orange polo shirt that was tucked inside of his pants. A worn belt from decades past complimented his wardrobe.

"You picked the wrong day. The wrong man," I offered with an impish smile on my face.

He poked me in the shoulder and said, "Why don't you mind your own damn business?"

I observed the hand that had just invaded my space. One of my favorite sayings came to mind. "You know something, mister. You just can't hide class," I said as I slid out of the booth.

We stood in front of each other and I could hear him breathing heavily. "Today is your day," I said.

"My day for what," he replied briskly as he raised his hand to poke me again.

"The day you think twice before making everyone around you miserable," and then I hit him so hard in the face with my right hand that I thought that I heard his jaw break at impact.

As I stood over him like Muhammad Ali in that

great photo where he towered over Sonny Liston. I thought about mimicking Ali gesturing at Liston to get up. I decided against that. One reason was because Ali was a national treasure and it would be sacrilege. Secondly, just like Liston, this guy wasn't getting up.

His wife stood and screamed as if I had committed an unpardonable offense. And I thought that she would be grateful. She began blotting the droplets of blood from his face with napkins. "Call 911!" she screamed as tears ran down her face. "Someone, please call 911!" she shouted again with a hysterical wail that grew in pitch.

I heard a lady behind me say, "Why?" People laughed and I thought I heard faint applause mixed in but that might of have been my imagination.

Thomas stood and gently pulled Angela with him. He held her hand with one hand and touched my shoulder with the other. "Time to depart," he said. He reached in his pocket and tossed sixty dollars on the table.

"You guys go," I said.

He hesitated and his eyes met mine. I nodded softly and smiled. "Go. No need for her vacation to be tied up. I'm good."

His expression was puzzled and he did not move. I nodded and winked at Angela. She pulled Thomas along with her and they walked to the door. Welcome to America, Angela, and springtime at Carolina Beach. I am reasonably certain that I will never see you again, but I bet a dollar to a Britt's donut you won't forget me.

The waitress touched my right hand. The man I had just decked with that same hand was regaining consciousness. He was moaning loudly and then I swear he began to cry. "Let me get you some ice for your hand," she said softly, smiling easily.

I stood motionless before turning back to look at the ogre of a man who was reduced to a crying baby. His wife looked up at me with tears streaming down her face. "Why did you hit him?"

I shook my head in disbelief.

"Why did you hit him?" she pleaded once again.

"Learn to stand up for yourself for God's sake."

"He was just hungry."

I shook my head with repulsion. "No, he is just an asshole."

"I think that you broke his jaw."

"I don't care," I deadpanned. "And if you had a brain, you would not care either."

"You don't understand."

"You got that right," I replied as I shook my head at another of life's great mysteries.

"Please come with me." The waitress said as she tugged on my left hand, hence to be known from this day forward as my jab hand now that I am a fighter. I looked into her soft brown eyes and nodded softly. We walked behind the counter and back into the kitchen. She led me past several members of the restaurant staff.

She pointed at the gunmetal gray door in the corner. "Leave through that door. Do you know your way around here?"

"I live within walking distance."

"I don't think I would go home just yet. Walk through those woods in back and keep walking diagonally to your right and you will wind up at the movie theater. Don't you think that it is a good afternoon for a movie?"

"My son worked there when he was in high school."

"Is your car here?"

"No. I rode with my friends."

"That's good."

She was as calm as the ocean on a windless morning in July. I love short women and she must have been about 5'2". She had a nice trim figure with just enough weight to be soft and sensuous.

"Stop staring at me and go," she said firmly.

"Thank you," I said as I pushed on the door. There was a small parking lot outside where employees parked. The woods were forty feet away. I turned back to her. It was warm and sunny as April is apt to be in southeastern North Carolina. "What about you? What are you going to say?"

"What kind of vehicle do you drive?"

"A black Toyota Tacoma."

"I am going to say that I went to get some ice for your hand and you ran out the back. I followed you long enough to see you drive away in a silver Honda Accord."

She had a nice southern accent with a hint still left of the country and there is a difference between a southern and country accent. If I have time, I may explain that later to my friends from the north.

"And how will you describe me?" I asked, while flashing my high voltage smile.

"Run of the mill," she answered without emotion. "An average Joe."

"Not even ruggedly handsome?" I countered in mock shock.

Try as she might she could not resist my charm. She broke down and grinned briefly. "Get out of here you idiot."

"You sure know how to talk to a man."

"Men are all the same," she replied, her voice heavier, and her beautiful eyes now distant and hollow. "They make empty promises when they feel good and cause grief the remainder of the time."

We both were outside the door now. The faint sound of sirens in the distance. "What is your name?"

"Ellie."

"Well Ellie, I am shocked that you would lump a man who has defended your honor against overwhelming odds as just another man." I looked at her with feigned hurt. Surely, she could not resist.

She couldn't and she broke into a grin. "Somehow, I fail to see where you were in any grave danger."

"He might have fallen on me. Did you even consider

that?" I responded quickly. I bet Ellie hasn't had this much intriguing dialogue in weeks, maybe years.

"No. I did not, Billy."

"You know my name."

"Of course, I do. Idiot. You told that guy you slugged your name."

"No, I did not. You overheard my companions say my name. You know why don't you? You are enthralled with me. Go ahead and admit it. You will feel so much better. It will be a weight off of your chest."

"Enthralled," she said, pretending to be shocked at my extensive grasp of the English language.

"It means…"

She responded by shoving me in the chest with both hands like Elaine often did on the sitcom *Seinfeld*. "I know what it means. Now get the hell out of here!"

I looked down and noticed the small wedding band on her finger. I've been single for a long time and you tend to notice these things, even when the cops are closing in.

My eyes returned to hers. She had caught me looking at her hand and she smiled in a knowing manner. "I guess I should go."

"Thank you. I have dealt with jerks like that my entire life and the man I married turned into one. It was nice to see one of them get what is coming to them just once."

Confident of my first victory in a fight in thirty years I made her an offer. "I could beat your husband up if you wish." I cocked my head slightly and smiled mischievously.

She dropped her head slightly as she tried to conceal the amusement on her face. It was impossible to do so and I knew that there was no way she could continue the charade of pretending to be unmoved by my allure. She looked back up and I noticed the contrast of how white her teeth were against the backdrop of her smooth olive complexion.

"Do you bleach your teeth regularly?"

She offered an expression of complete disbelief. I have that effect on people.

I shrugged my shoulders. "You know it is not good if you bleach them too frequently."

Her stare led me to believe that she is not the least bit interested in my concern about her dental health. It is frustrating to try to help people and be ignored.

"They are pretty and next to your skin..."

"Please go," she said wearily. "I don't want to get caught up in all of this."

"But you already are since I came to your rescue."

"Rescue? He wasn't going to hit me."

"He wasn't going to hit me either," I responded quickly like a third-grader at recess.

It is the natural progression of life as we grow older for many of us to desire to reach back to our youth. The simple things we treasured. Model trains, a day at the beach, collecting baseball cards, playing whatever sport was in season on the fields in Sea Gate.

Perhaps we should return to our childhood to solve disputes such as the one Ellie and I are currently having. Nothing like a good argument between third graders to simplify our complex lives.

"You are so full of yourself."

I breathed deeply as those words took me to a place I did not care to visit. It was a time not long ago when a woman I loved at a time I had given up on love said that same line to me often. She always said it with a smile on her face. Sadness washed over me and a pain that could not be healed just yet emerged.

My eyes found their way back to Ellie. She stared intently.

I shook my head, annoyed with myself that I could not hide the pain of a simple statement. Big tough guy like me, a fighter for the love of Pete. But then nothing can bring a man to his knees like the love of a woman.

"Will you please leave?" she softly pleaded.

I flashed my B smile at her. Believe it or not, it appeared to have no effect. "Shouldn't we kiss or something? You know like in the movies when the guy saves the gal and they are never going to see each other again."

"What tacky movie would that be?" she asked as she struggled not to be moved by my copious charm. I admired her attempted resistance. It would never work but the commitment to such a bold stand was indeed honorable.

"Several I bet but right now I can't concentrate because you are so cute."

She took my compliment as serenely as if I had said the weather sure was nice. Unbelievable.

"You think I might be lucky enough not to see you again?" she stated flatly.

Before I could think of a witty response, she put both hands on my upper chest, which is really one of my better body parts, and shoved me firmly against the wall. She moved in swiftly and kissed me hard with either passion or anger. I am not certain of which. Maybe a combination of the two.

"Now go," she said as she turned me and shoved me toward the woods, and walked back inside, closing the door behind her.

The police were now probably in the parking lot out front judging from the increased decibels of the sirens. I slowly recovered from the shock of having her tongue shoved down my throat. Realizing that it was indeed time to depart, I recalled something similar to what Forrest Gump once said, "It seemed like a fine idea." I walked briskly through the parking lot and entered the woods. There was a worn narrow path and I began walking in the general direction of the movie theater.

I was no more than twenty-five feet into the woods when I heard the back door to the restaurant open harshly. I squatted down behind a dense mass of Yaupon

Holly trees and watched. There were two officers. One was about my age and the other was young. As young as the punk city cop, with an arrogant attitude, that gave me a ticket on Hooker Road last week. Hooker Road, that's right. I did not make it up. Wilmington, the city that makes up the larger portion of New Hanover County, of which Carolina Beach is part of, has a road named Hooker. The sign was stolen so habitually that now it seems to be about twenty feet high. It helped but not long ago I read where someone sawed the metal pole into and took the sign and the pole.

I watched Ellie follow them out the door. I licked my lips absently and tasted her kiss. What would she do? She pointed to her left and while I could not hear what was being said, I knew she was telling them about a car I did not possess—driving in a direction that I was not going. Minutes later the three of them walked back inside. I rose and continued my journey.

Twenty minutes later I was inside the Cinema Four. I chose an action flick to pass the time. A sudden thought hit me. Didn't they catch Lee Harvey Oswald in the movie theater?

Considering what a pretty day it was the worn room contained only an older couple, me, and a lot of empty seats. The movie was one of the many average movies Hollywood produced. I longed for the times my son, Micah and I, watched a movie and he immediately gave his critical review upon leaving the theater.

What a gig it must be to get paid to critique movies. It requires no real qualifications and all you really need to do is pick some mediocre movie and make it out to be great art that a less intelligent person is not capable of grasping. And don't get me started on Tom Cruise being some superhuman action star.

§

It was late afternoon as I walked through the woods in the direction of my house. The road would have proven easier but walking in the woods this time of year is not such a bad thing and when you consider the cops may be looking for me—probably the wiser choice to be on the narrow trail that I am.

I guess now would be a good idea to explain to you how Micah came into the equation. Soon after my divorce, I drunkenly slept several times with a college girl and that produced Micah. His mother, Tiffany and I had no intention of a relationship forming. Fortunately, being raised in a strict Catholic home, she did not consider abortion, and even better for me, she did not want a child inhibiting her life. She signed over full custody with the written promise that she absolved any rights to him and wanted assurances that he would never be allowed to contact her. I also assumed the entire financial responsibility of raising him. Aided by the help of close friends and family, Micah was raised by all of us. We gave love and unconditional support but he gave us so much more.

You might be wondering if I had a paternity test done after my previous debacle. I did, though I felt foolish to have done so. He was my son right down to the exact shape of his eyes. Only the color was different. His were a deep brown that showed tenderness unmatched in my world.

His mom moved back out west where she was from. Are you sensing a pattern here? Micah as a small child never showed any interest in where his mother was that I observed and I was on full alert for any such signs.

Tiffany reappeared when he was seven years old and decided that along with the help of her affluent parents, she wanted to not only be involved in the child's life who she abandoned but sought sole custody and wanted to move him out west. I could have him each summer.

Their dream team of attorneys told the court that this entire episode was my fault. I seduced a young college girl and pressured her into signing documents, waiving her rights as a parent.

There indeed was seduction but it was the other way around and it was all her idea to sign the papers. But the truth gets muddied when people cannot be honest when their gaze in the mirror is confronted by unpleasant facts.

It was an ugly custody battle and I spent my savings fighting for the child that had known only me as a parent and was doing quite well. The final verdict was to share custody and now my time with my son was reduced to

Thursday afternoon till Sunday night when I had to make the long drive to Brunswick County to return him.

The judge did at least deny my child being moved from this area. Her parents thought that was a preposterous decision because they could give my son all the things that I could not. My judicious mom said at the time, "*It is easier for a camel to go through the eye of a needle than for someone who is rich to enter the kingdom of God.*" Mom told me after the court battle to pray for Tiffany and her parents. I told her tersely to go to hell. It was not one of my prouder moments. Thankfully mom's grace is without limits. She accepted my apology the next day—understanding that I was just lashing out in frustration.

Micah, for the most part, adjusted well and they formed what appeared to be a healthy relationship. Tiffany never worked and was handed everything by her parents. My child, who never cared about material things, now had the latest toys, clothes, electronics, you name it, and I could not compete with that. All I could do was try to teach him that people were what was important and that things were perishable at best.

I stopped at the edge of the woods that bordered my neighborhood. There was not a police car in sight in my cul-de-sac. I had not searched for police cars since the days of my youth when I sold marijuana. I was quite successful at it if you don't count that one time my so-called best friend ratted me out to save his sorry ass from going to prison. He died a few years ago from hepatitis contracted during another of his many bouts with heroin addiction. It could not have happened to a more deserving guy. My only hope is that he did not die quickly.

I walked casually to my house and went inside. I was almost disappointed that I had not had to sneak past a squad of police cars. Maybe Ellie did not tell them how handsome I am. "That's it," I said, comforting my ego, as I removed a Pacifico beer from the fridge. The sound of my voice seemed to echo off the high ceilings. I opened the beer and drank half of it. I plopped down on the couch and clicked the television on. Clint Eastwood filled the screen in *Dirty Harry*. Ah Clint, now there was a certified action star if there ever was one.

I watched Clint shoot someone and I thought that perhaps tonight would be a good night to start the DVD box set I purchased a year ago that was still in the wrapper. All five movies with Callahan carrying a handgun as long as my arm and a dry wit that offered one-liners with the ease of a Nolan Ryan fastball.

My stomach rumbled and I remembered that I had not eaten since lunch. There was pork tenderloin in the fridge that had been marinating in George's Barbeque Sauce. It is my top go-to barbeque sauce. Most of the big-name sauces begin with sugar and go downhill from there. I discovered George's at the local Food Lion on the beach and decided at once to stop my futile attempts of trying to create my own. My pattern of the past weeks has been to plan to cook dinner before discarding my plan once I saw bagels in the fridge and knew there was peanut butter in the cabinet. Cooking for one person is not much fun and even less so of late. I searched the fridge for everything I needed, and in the process, realized that I was out of bagels anyway.

I walked to the garage and placed the grill just outside the door. I positioned the charcoal starter in the grill and filled it with charcoal. Next, I shoved two wadded pieces of newspaper underneath the starter and lit the paper. My world like most people these days is lived at too fast a pace. I try to win small battles. One is that I refuse to buy a gas grill for convenience. Besides, it tastes better with charcoal, doesn't it? Even if it doesn't, I like lighting the coals and watching them get ready. I slid a white Adirondack chair a few feet from the grill and rested in it on the open front porch. After several minutes, the coals glowed with red flames. I dumped the coals into the grill and put the grate in place.

I walked back inside and sliced some squash, zucchini, and a few mushrooms. Next, I poured some olive oil into a bowl and rubbed each piece in it, and then slid it on a skewer. I sprinkled Cavender's, a wonderful Greek seasoning that goes well on about anything, along with salt and some fancy coarse ground pepper. Now I can't tell you if this pepper is better than the cheap stuff but it makes me feel like a real chef. Forget flowers, nothing speaks to a woman's heart like watching a man in the kitchen cook for her. I always like to keep their wine glass full while I am cooking because I think I look even better after a few glasses. No woman tonight. I was alone and I should be used to that by now. I have had my share of relationships and most were short lived. Sometimes my choice and sometimes theirs. My last one of any length was with Jada. It ended last summer. We lasted ten months. Damn close to a record. She was a nice girl but really demanding toward the end. I got really tired of that really quick.

Thoughts of the lady I dated briefly back in the fall that use to tell me I was so full of myself surfaced but I willed the thoughts away the best I could. I walked inside to retrieve another beer and paused to look around at the emptiness of my house. It is a funny thing about being alone. If there is no one in my life. It grows old quickly but if there is someone, I savor every moment of solitude. Ah, we all want what we do not have. The grass is always greener elsewhere.

I walked back to the garage. The grill was ready and I placed the meat that I had wrapped in tin foil on the Weber grill along with the skewer.

The sun was setting slightly off to my right. The orange light flickered through the oak trees across the street. The neighbor's Husky was outside on the second-story porch and bellowed with his distinctive howl. The glass door opened and he disappeared. Frequently

this time of day I would ride my bike into the nearby
Carolina Beach State Park. Often, I have had to stop
and allow the deer to cross the road. I would pause at
the end of the road where the marina was and watch the
sun bed down over the river. Tonight, I felt more like
cooking and drinking beer. Well, at least I felt more like
drinking beer.

The ice-cold beer felt good in my right hand. My
power punching hand. My knuckles were slightly
swollen and there was a bruise forming. I went back
inside and placed ice in a small Ziplock bag. I walked
back to the garage, sat, and positioned the bag of ice on
my hand. Typically, I would be reading a fictional book
of some sort as I grilled but I didn't feel like it. Lately, I
had begun reading the Spenser novels by Robert Parker.
He died a few years back but he left behind forty novels
of the wisecracking Spenser. I have read about ten of
them and there are plenty to go. Once I read a quote that
reading reminds us that we are not alone. I don't know
who said it but it is a pretty astute statement.

I thought about the long-ago *Spenser* television
show. Robert Urich, now that was a handsome man. I
debated briefly as to whether he was better looking than
I. It is close but I have to give him the nod. Pains me to
do so but these things must be as they are.

Jada criticized me in our last conversation for reading
too much. In my usual charming way when I have had
enough of someone's crap I replied, "Yeah, better to

sneak off and have a smoke with the girls like you do. That is the healthier way to unwind."

She hid her little habit from me the best she could. Still, alcohol tends to make us all less alert. We met some friends of hers from work one night at a bar on the Island. She made several trips to the bathroom with her boss. Only an old man has to urinate that frequently.

As we were leaving that night, I turned to her and asked, "So, how long have you been a closet smoker?"

She struggled to say something in return but the shock on her face, followed by resignation spoke louder than words.

It became a wonderful conversation topic and in time despite her assurances that I was just the reason she needed to quit for good I knew that she had no intention of doing so. It was okay. Smoke'em if you got'em because by then we had more problems than her sneaking off like a seventh-grader to light up with girlfriends.

Is it any wonder that relationships fail at such a dramatic rate? People begin with lies of one kind or another. Once during a particularly frustrating time, I briefly tried online dating. Why would someone say they were slim when they were fifty pounds overweight? Did they think I was blind or is it that the mirrors in their home just don't function properly?

I met her at a coffee shop. I was as nice as I could be for as long as I could be. That was for about ten minutes. "The photo you put on your profile was from how long ago?" I inquired.

Her face narrowed. Not as much as chicken man but you get the idea. "What do you mean by that?"

I was in it now but I wasn't the one who used a photo from several years ago and lied about my current shape. "I just think these online meetings might go better if we were honest. Like you saying that you are slim."

That did it. "You are a horrible man," she lashed out as she stood up, adjusting her jeans that were two sizes too small as she did.

"But I am honest."

Indignant, she grabbed her Elvis purse from the table knocking the cup of coffee to the floor as she did. I waited several minutes as people snuck looks at me, trying to muster enough dignity to leave. Also, I wanted to make sure she had cleared the parking lot.

My thoughts drifted away from Elvis and back to Jada. Funny thing about women is that whatever they really like about you initially will when it all goes to hell use the same thing to criticize you for. In the beginning, it was so cool that she had a boyfriend that actually read. And in the end, well, suffice to say that it was not so good.

I removed the skewer and slid the veggies into the bowl. A few minutes passed and I began to sample them and rapidly consumed the contents.

My thoughts drifted to my son. He always had a love and passion for drama and that is the reason the video case that I built that stands in the living room, would do a small Mom and Pop video rental justice if those places still existed today.

Micah went to college at the University of North Carolina at Greensboro at the age of seventeen. He graduated two years ago and is living in New York, trying out for every part he can on Broadway. He has gotten a few small parts and he works as a waiter while he pursues that one big break.

Tiffany, well you might not believe this story but bear in mind one of my favorite sayings 'truth is stranger than fiction.' Micah rarely spoke of his mom around me. He was always an insightful kid and he knew the pain in my heart each time I had to leave him in the wealthy gated community where his mom resided.

He was fifteen when he shared that his mom rarely stayed at home the nights that he was with her. Perhaps, sensing that their daughter was going off the rails once again, her mom had temporarily moved in the castle that she and her husband had purchased for their errant unproductive child. He told me that he did not want to return. My son was asking me to rescue him. I wish it were that simple. I had not the financial means to even explore taking on another custody battle against her wealthy family. I asked him to give me some time, but for now, he had to continue to adhere to the court-mandated schedule.

I shared this information with mom during one of

our almost daily phone calls. It was the following day when dad called and asked if I could blow the leaves off the roof of their home. As he had gotten older, he was not as confident about climbing the ladder and walking on the roof.

I went to my parents' home that afternoon. Did I mention that my dad is the most impatient man on earth so if I did not get to it quickly, he would be on the roof? No one wanted that.

There were but a scant few leaves on the roof and I was done in ten minutes. As I was coming down the ladder dad was waiting and I knew this afternoon was not about removing debris from the roof.

He watched as I put the ladder away and it was not like him to go this long without speaking. If nothing else he would typically tell me the correct way to put the ladder away but he remained silent. His expression reminded me of a lost child in the woods—unsure of which path led to home. "Got something on your mind, Pop?"

He still did not speak.

"Mom, okay?"

He nodded.

"Dad, I never knew you to be short on words," I said with a slight grin.

He smiled slightly and nodded once again. I waited for him to speak.

He reached into his pocket and pulled a check out

along with a business card and handed them to me. I did not look at what was in my hand.

"Dad?" His eyes failed to meet mine. "Dad?"

He refused to raise his eyes and slowly he began to speak. "Your mom told me about Micah not wanting to go to that bitch's house that caused all this trouble. She and those rich ass parents of hers think they are better than everyone." He breathed in deeply and said, "Micah is better off with you and not just because she is a bitch. You are a good dad. He worships the ground you walk on." He turned and walked inside never once able to look me in the eyes.

I stood there perplexed for several moments before I looked in my hand. The business card was for a prominent attorney. Mom shared later that dad had grown up with him. They had not spoken since they played baseball together during their last year of high school. The two boys from Fifth and Castle took different routes. Dad became a career police officer and Crawford Hollister became a well-known attorney.

I would discover later that dad had reached out to him and Crawford remembered dad fondly from the days of their youth. Still, he was an expensive attorney and pro bono work was not exactly something he took part in. But he did tell dad he would receive the family discount and he assured him that if the facts of this case were true, he would indeed win.

There were two things as I stood in my parents'

backyard that day that astounded me. The first was that the check was made out to the firm of Crawford Hollister for twenty thousand dollars. The even more surprising matter was that the scraggly signature of the check belonged to my dad. Mom did all the banking in our family. She wrote the checks and paid the bills. Dad got spending money and he was happy with the arrangement. He never wrote checks.

I started to go inside but I stopped. Dad wanted no part of being thanked. Not right now. I respected that and I got in my truck and drove away.

Oh, the truth is stranger than fiction part. We never had to go to court. Two months later Tiffany was pregnant again. This time by a nineteen-year-old freshman from the local university. It was kind of hard to blame this one on me.

The day when I got my son back for good. Let me tell you about that triumph. Crawford sat at the head of the long, sleek mahogany table that was polished to the point that there were slight reflections of the people seated at the table. Crawford wore a dark gray suit that was as smooth as the graceful wood in front of us. His salt and pepper hair expertly trimmed. His fingernails manicured smartly. He obviously had come a long way from Fifth and Castle Street.

I was seated to his right. Tiffany, her parents, and three high profile attorneys sat across from us. Despite what Tiffany's father was paying the attorneys I knew his arrogance would not allow them to speak solely on the matter. He would expect to have this issue resolved to his liking.

Crawford began our meeting by opening a folder and passing eight by ten photos of Tiffany's excursions to her parents and their attorneys.

The mom gasped, especially at the picture of her precious Tiffany bending over a table in a nightclub wearing a skirt so short you could see her red, lace, thong underwear. Even worse was what she was doing as she leaned over the table. There was a rolled-up bill with Franklin's picture, inserted up one nostril as she greedily snorted the white powder on the table.

Tiffany's dad, though shaken for the moment was still intent on things being resolved to his liking. He recovered quickly and began speaking in his rich, practiced voice despite his lead attorney's advice to be quiet. "Okay, for today it appears that you may have won. Micah is fifteen so this will be the following arrangement. He will return to your primary custody and he will spend the summers out west with us. We are taking our daughter home to help her." He actually stood up as if the meeting was over.

The arrogance in his tone pushed me over the edge and I was rising out of my chair when I felt Crawford's strong grip hold me in check. Dude may well be the age of my father but man he had an authoritative grip.

Crawford studied the man for several moments.

"No," he stated evenly. The two men stared intently at each other.

"There's more, Mr. Kennedy," Crawford stated assuredly as he opened his laptop and began clicking the mouse. He turned the video of my son in the direction of the opposing counsel.

I could not see his face but I could hear my son's voice. "I asked my dad three months ago to not make me go to Tiffany's house any longer."

Tiffany visibly flinched at hearing her name spoken by my son. She had lost the right to be addressed as mom.

"I knew I was asking a lot of my dad and I knew it was not that simple. But I know my dad and he is the one that has always been there for me. His nightlife was never more significant than me. Nothing in his life has been as important as I am.

"I wish to reside with my dad until I am of legal age and this court, which so foolishly screwed up the custody battle eight years ago, will then have no saying in my life. And this is my life, in case judges, attorneys, and my grandparents on Tiffany's side have forgotten or more likely never recognized in the first place.

"Tiffany, you have been caught with your pants down so to speak once again. Will you also place the blame on my dad for this as well? Go back to your home. I pray you get help. As a much younger child, I was swayed by all the luxury your parents bestowed upon me. I am a little older now and I see clearly that my dad has always offered the far greater riches.

"Grandfather, before you demand I spend the summers out west-knowing full well you will spend that time to encourage me to attend college near you, let me state that the answer is unequivocally no.

"Tiffany, I am not angry with you. You are a product of your unfortunate upbringing or lack thereof. I wish you well. But go home and clean your life up. Maybe you can be the mom to this child that you could not be to me. Maybe one day if you turn your life around, we can talk. Maybe even have a relationship but that day is not today.

"I belong with my dad. I should have fought harder for him. It shames me that I did not."

There was a silence at the table that is beyond any quiet that I have ever known. I think it astonished everyone at the table but me that a fifteen-year-old could speak so eloquently and factually. I was not surprised because my son has always had an old soul residing inside of him.

The next words spoken were by Tiffany. "Micah is right." She rose and walked out of our lives. Her father sat without motion as he searched for words that would somehow turn this bitter defeat around.

Crawford closed his laptop and gathered his files. And as he did so he remarked, "It appears you are no longer calling the shots, Mr. Kennedy."

Tiffany's father stood and narrowed his eyes in my direction. "I could have given Micah so much more than the likes of someone like you."

"It is very sad that even after hearing my son speak that you actually believe that."

He cursed under his breath, snorted angrily, rose and walked out hurriedly as if he were trying to outpace defeat. Crawford and I sat there for several moments relishing in quiet victory. We could hear Tiffany's dad screaming at the attorneys for their failure to win.

My very professional attorney then did something that surprised me. He held out his fist for a fist bump which I complied with. "Call your dad and put him on speaker phone." I did so.

"Hello."

"Dad. We won. It's over."

"Without even going to court?"

"Let's say that Crawford was able to find some damning evidence on Tiffany."

"Well, I'll be. I can't believe it."

Crawford was grinning as he touched my arm. "Bill, Crawford here. I told you that I would kick his ass. And we have a new deal. I am going to refund your money."

I shook my head in dismay and my father was quiet.

"Why?" Dad finally asked.

"I am impressed with your son and even more so your grandson. I understand he desires a career in acting but as a fallback plan he could be an attorney. He sure speaks a lot better than we did at that age.

"Here is the new deal. You can take me to dinner at that barbeque place in Sea Gate. We will bring our wives."

"I guess I can afford that."

"Bill, I am refunding your twenty thousand dollars."

"I was joking, Crawford," my dad said dryly and they both fell into laughter that childhood friends can so easily slip into.

They would meet at that barbeque restaurant monthly for the next three years, before Dad passed away. Crawford served as one of the pall bearers.

The call ended and we remained seated. I searched for words of gratitude but what words in the English language could possibly exist when speaking of the saving of one's child? The lead opposing attorney suddenly entered the room and closed the door behind him.

He was dressed smoothly in a dark blue suit. A yellow handkerchief was neatly placed in his coat pocket matching his patterned tie that contained stripes of the same color.

"Off the record, Crawford?"

"Sure thing, Daniel."

Daniel looked at me. "I am glad that you won. That smug bastard," he said with a shake of his head. He reached his hand out to me and I stood and shook it. "I wish you and your son the very best."

"Thank you."

He turned and walked away. "For what? This never happened." He exited through the door as his words trailed behind him.

"Crawford, I don't know where to begin."

He shook his head. "Don't." And then he laughed. "I was going to win regardless but my wife is the primary reason I refused payment. I usually don't talk to her about cases but this one got to me a bit as I delved into it. We have grandchildren near the age of Micah. She said to me. "Crawford, you get that boy back with his daddy. And don't charge your old friend a penny. We have been blessed with more than we will ever need in this lifetime." He sighed before adding, "I am only the boss here."

I envied his tone and his slight smile. He was obviously content with his wife having her way.

He pushed a button on a machine near him. "Stephanie, please bring the good stuff."

Stephanie entered the room and placed a whiskey decanter and two old fashioned glasses on the table in front of him. "I am not pouring." She walked away in a business-like fashion.

"Don't forget that I am your boss."

She stuck her head back in the room. "Don't forget that you would be lost without me."

He chuckled softly and said, "Well, at least I thought I was in charge here. He poured two fingers in each glass.

We held our glass up to each other and slightly touched them. The bourbon was full bodied, with a hint of vanilla. Hell, I am just kidding you. I got no idea if it has vanilla in it or not. Let's just state that it is far smoother and cost way more than all the spirits combined in my little liquor cabinet at home. We sipped in silence for several moments. Both of us reveling in our victory. He placed his empty glass on the table. "Lot better stuff than your dad and I snuck away to drink in high school."

§

When the meat was ready, I took it inside and ate over half of it. Then I put everything away and cleaned up. I put the first Dirty Harry movie in the player and stretched out in my recliner. It was three in the morning, and I was watching the fourth movie when I finally nodded off to sleep. Clint must have shot a dozen people by now. Imagine that. Tom Cruise would still be fumbling to pull his gun from his holster.

MONDAY

We were sitting on the porch of the house that was constructed when I was one year old. Mom was once again explaining how God had a plan for my life and that the best part was yet to come. I often debated with her about how much God was involved in our daily life but it granted her comfort to believe he is right here with us in every decision so I refrained from challenging her beliefs. God is in control as I have often heard from her and other staunch Christians. When I hear that phrase, I still think of 911 and the heat so intense in the twin towers that people leapt to their death. All of this caused by cowardly, evil men, and I can't help but wonder just where God was on that day. In control of this world—I struggle with that concept.

As I bask in the warmth of mom's voice a thumping sound invades the tranquility of the moment. It grows louder and I strain to hear what she is saying. Her voice faded to a whisper and I reached out for her. "Mom, don't go yet," I pleaded and then I woke with a start. The sheets drenched in sweat. Off in the distance, I hear the pounding noise again and the realization that the rhythmic sound being produced is that of a nail gun. The intrusive clamor is in all likelihood coming from the house that is being built just outside of our neighborhood. The pulsating sound seems to be in tune with the pounding that is taking place inside my head.

I rose briefly and a wave of nausea swept over me. Feeling like this is why these days I typically cease drinking after three or four beers, which I did not do last night. Maybe it would have been better to stick to my routine. Either that or go back to drinking all the time. I laid back down. It was far too early in the day to be trying to decipher just what a proper drinking pattern might be.

I looked at my watch. It was just before nine. Another thought hits me that I am late for work. That thought is followed by the first good consideration of the day. I sold my landscaping business two weeks ago. Currently I am either unemployed or on vacation. You decide. The business netted someone with limited financial needs such as me a tidy little sum. I plan to take off for the remainder of spring and summer. Maybe by fall I will know what it is that I aspire to do when I grow up, which seems less likely to transpire with each passing day.

I marshaled some willpower and rose gingerly. I rested for a moment as I sat on the edge of the bed. I reflected on my possible criminal status and walked to the window—moving the curtains to the side and peeking out—relieved to see the neighborhood was going about a routine Monday morning. Translation being there were no police cars except on the street behind me, which was normal because Dennis, the cop resided there. I closed the curtain and walked to the bathroom. I reached for my head as if that will stop the throbbing and realized that my right hand ached in harmony with the pounding in my head. It takes me a moment to remember why it hurts. That is right. I am a tough guy. A tough guy who just woke from the darkness of a dream wanting his mama.

I used the bathroom, washed my hands like mom taught me when I was very little, and walked to the kitchen and started the coffee.

I stepped outside on the porch to check out the weather. It was a beautiful sunny day and warm enough for the beach. A neighbor who walked his Beagle every morning rain or shine was entering the cul-de-sac. He raised his hand and waved and I did likewise. One thing that I looked forward to with no job schedule to adhere to is working out in the mornings when none of the cool people wearing their jungle gym pants and muscle shirts frequented the gym. They were present in the late afternoon and early evening like clockwork. Some people referred to that time as meat market time, but I preferred the less harsh term of beautiful people time. It is probably because I coined that particular phrase. I might miss watching some of the newcomers join the gym that believe it pertinent to start dressing the part before they see physical results. There is nothing quite like the sight of a tall skinny kid, weighing in at one-hundred and forty pounds, with toothpick arms, and he is already donning sleeveless shirts.

Mornings at the gym are for the most part filled with retirees and full-time moms who have dropped their kids off at school. That is more my speed these days. Maybe it was the beers that I drank last night, but I do not feel motivated to drive to the gym to lift weights. I decided the beach was the better option. After breakfast of course. It is the most important meal of the day. Mom taught me that as well right before she placed five pieces of French toast, slathered in butter and syrup in front of me. All those calories and still as a child I was so rail thin a slight breeze could blow me over.

I scrambled three eggs and mixed in a little pepperjack cheese. The coffee was ready and I added stevia and half and half. My sainted mom drank coffee black every morning for as long as I can recall and I don't know how. She compounded her error by drinking instant coffee.

I ate breakfast and drank coffee while watching SportsCenter. I finished breakfast—set the plate on the table beside me and channel surfed for a few minutes. As I searched for a worthwhile channel with my trusty remote, I recalled a story about my dad. He always referred to the remote as the clicker and he became extremely agitated if his clicker was not close by his right hand. Sometimes when he had fallen asleep in his recliner, I would hide his prized clicker and leave. The best clicker prank was the day that I walked into the living room and found him snoring away in the recliner. Mom was not home. The precious clicker lay on the armrest. I lifted it carefully, hid it in the refrigerator behind an antique piece of orange Tupperware from 1985. My parents threw nothing away. I departed as quietly as a baseball field proved to be in winter.

He asked me later if I had come by that day. I played dumb, which considering many of the decisions I have made in my life is not much of an achievement. He never mentioned the clicker. He probably suspected his absent-mindedness as much as he did me playing a practical joke on him. Mom told me later that he tore the house apart for the rest of the day before she found it when she retrieved leftovers for dinner. She didn't ask me if I did it. She probably did not want to know or more likely she knew the culprit was her favorite child and wanted as she always did to keep things peaceful.

A few minutes later I am driving to the beach. In the back of my truck is a beach chair that is so worn it might snap into at any moment, along with my backpack that is equipped with the needed beach items. A book, towel, sunscreen, and bottled water.

The traffic light in front of me turned red and being the law-abiding citizen that I am, I stopped. The car in front of me is a white Nissan Sentra. The car wiggled sporadically. Intrigued I attempted to decipher the mystery. "Ah," I say.

The woman driving this car is large. I can tell this because part of her anatomy is encroaching into the console area. The wiggling I detected is her attempt to adjust her seat belt. She seems quite aggravated and snatched it. The car wiggled again. She needs to either lose weight or buy a bigger car.

I speculated as to what type of automobile my buddy from yesterday drives. There was no way that he could fit into an economy car. I bet he prefers a very large car to drive in his pursuit of the next buffet, which I don't think he will be partaking in for quite some time as I know of no liquid buffets that you can suck through a straw. It brings a smile to my face and love in my heart to think about his not being able to eat solid food for weeks.

Bored with the plump woman I looked at the car beside her. It was a full-size truck with a personalized license plate with a combination of numbers and letters. Despite my high degree of intelligence; I don't have a clue as to what it means. Why do people do that? If it is not readable—what is the point? I shook my head and made a near-fatal mistake. I glanced at the car beside me.

The woman behind the wheel has puffed platinum blonde hair that might be touching the roof. Her hair appeared every bit as natural as one of those old commercials where people losing their hair spray painted the thin spots. She smacked her lips together which were coated in shocking pink lipstick. She placed one hand on the wheel and in the other hand; she was holding a Styrofoam cup of coffee and a lit cigarette between her index and middle finger. Talk about multitasking.

As I watched in amazement, I concluded that if you started your day with a smoke and coffee. That has to be the high point. The day can't get any better, right? A hundred bucks says she wears perfume that you can smell for miles. Two hundred says she has leopard clothing somewhere on her body. I frequently astonished myself with such shrewd perceptions. And this coming from a man whose head felt so dense that it is like the blackened fog in a horror movie right before a grotesque hand reached out and snatched their prey.

Being the judicious observer that you are, I bet you know where this is going and are laughing at my obvious mistake. As I am wearing my hands out patting myself on the back for my clever perceptions, I have failed to notice that Blondie has observed me looking her way. She smiled and arched her eyes suggestively. I smiled faintly and returned to looking at the white car in front of me. Okay, I admit it. I am a little afraid.

The light finally changed. Is it my imagination or did it take ten minutes? She tooted the horn and waved. I tell you being this good-looking is not always the perk people might deem it to be. I am not safe even at a traffic light. I drove on but at a slower pace than her.

I parked in a nearly vacant lot. I gathered my things out of the truck bed and walked toward the beach. To my left is one of the remaining motels that offered inexpensive weekly and monthly rentals during the off season. Carolina Beach was once labeled as a redneck beach and while that was for the most part a false rap—it doesn't mean that there are not a few good old boys who grace us with their charm. One such man was standing on the second-floor balcony smoking a cigarette. He wore cut off blue jeans that I bet you served as a bathing suit as well. It chaffed my inner thighs just to entertain such a notion.

I recalled a bike ride this past winter that took me

past the same motel where this distinguished gentleman is currently residing. It was Saturday—a little past six a.m. and I observed a woman tossing a mattress and other items from the second floor down to the parking lot. I thought it was kind of a peculiar time to be moving and the method seemed a little unorthodox, though it did cut down on the time using the steps required.

I continued on my bike ride along Carolina Beach Avenue North to the end of the street by the pier and looped back down Canal Street. As I biked back by the same motel fifteen minutes later there were two police cars, and a disgruntled man dressed in jeans and no shirt, looking at his clothes lying on top of the mattress. The woman, obviously done with her early morning housecleaning was nowhere in sight.

I heard a voice from above. "Morning, buddy."

"Good morning," I responded pleasantly as I continued walking without interruption.

I managed a few steps beyond him when it dawned on me that I am wearing a Wrightsville Beach tee shirt from their annual flotilla. The writing on the front is barely visible from a distance but the back has a large logo on it. For a long time, there was a kind of civil unrest between the two coastal towns that are fifteen miles apart. Wrightsville Beach held the richer properties while Carolina Beach was viewed as more of a working man's beach, though as Bob Dylan crooned; "The Times They Are A-Changing." The truth is there are many things to love about both beaches. Wrightsville Beach has a cleaner ocean in appearance most days because it does not have the Cape Fear River to contend with as Carolina Beach does. Carolina Beach has more undeveloped land—including Carolina Beach State Park, which has over seven hundred acres of land that mainly consisted of woods. It was also a more efficient place to live. You can purchase almost anything you need without leaving the Island. Forget about that at Wrightsville, where much of the commercial property had been rezoned to residential because the owners and developers could make more money.

But things have changed and you don't hear that kind of talk so much these days. "Wrightsville Beach," he uttered with an air of disdain. "What are you doing at Carolina Beach?" Indubitably there are exceptions to any rule.

Just keep walking and ignore the ignorant man I heard my rational voice say. And then an image of a woman flashed in my mind. Why at this moment I did not know but that was all it took. I turned and retraced my steps. The sneer on his face vanished—replaced with trepidation. God help me but I was going to prey on that.

"I'm minding my own business. Why don't you try doing the same?"

"Wrightsville Beach," he muttered as he shook his head in disgust.

I offered my very best smart-ass smile as I motioned for him to come on down. He swallowed heavily and struggled to reply. His mouth began to move again, but I quickly cut him off.

"I'm not interested in having a conversation, however intellectually stimulating it might prove to be with someone of your obvious acumen. You can walk down the steps and we can settle this right here in the parking lot. Or you can turn around walk back inside and later you can get drunk and lie to your buddies about how you ran some Wrightsville Beach dude away."

He struggled to say something but his brain and mouth were not dancing in rhythm together. As long as it was taking him to formulate what he wanted to say the dance had to be a slow one. He considered his options for several moments.

I held my hands out to my side with my palms up.

Meekly, he turned toward the door and disappeared inside. I felt a twinge of sorrow for him. Well, maybe it was less than a twinge but what word would that be? I didn't have a clue.

As I continued walking to the beach it is beginning to dawn on me just what being tough actually is. It is being fearless about what could happen to you. Maybe in my case, my soul has been tormented and pillaged for the last time. Tormented and pillaged? That is rather harsh thinking for so early in the morning.

I walked past a few people on the Boardwalk. I did

my best not to frighten anyone. I even smiled at a little blonde-haired girl whose mom had pinned her curly hair on top of her head. She smiled back. The poor child is too young to know what a dangerous man I am.

I have a ritual when I go to the beach. Rarely do I sit in my chair first. I set my chair up, unload my stuff, take my shirt off and dive into the ocean. Although, I know the April water is a little chilly I see no reason to stray from my routine.

I walked toward the ocean. Never do I run. That is for a tourist or a young kid wanting to show off. It's kind of pointless to run to dive into the ocean. It is not as if it is going anywhere.

I waded in and ignored the cold. The water temperature was probably around sixty-two degrees. The ocean floor dropped off quickly and the water was up to my chest. I love the sea but I am respectful of it. One false move has cost many a person their life. I gauged the time in between waves and moved quickly after one passed and dove before the following wave could break on me. I come up for air and immersed myself in God's greatest creation once again. That is enough for now. I returned to my beach chair and sat. My head slightly clearer. I removed a bottle of water and pulled out a Robert Parker novel from my backpack. Thirty minutes later I put it aside and fell asleep with the sun basking on my skin.

"There he is." I opened my eyes. Three men are standing in front of me. In the middle is the man I had the pleasure of conversing with earlier. The other two appeared to be his brothers. The one to my right looked as if he was the oldest and the one to my left the youngest. I guess I was doomed, considering there was a trio of morons in front of me.

"Hi, boys," I offered cheerfully.

"Get up," the oldest instructed.

I did as he ordered with a huge smile.

I looked at my earlier acquaintance. "Wow. Triple the fun. What's the matter? Don't you have any sisters?"

The oldest spoke again. "That's right. Be cute. My brother says you started some trouble with him when he was just being friendly."

"That is correct," I answered swiftly. "That is exactly what I did," I said as I looked squarely at the brother in the middle. His face was masked with confusion. He had a nice story to weave and now he had no need of it. Probably his brainpower for the week shot to hell and unnecessarily so. Gee, how I hated to disrupt his plans. "Let me guess. Now you good ole boys are going to make sure I pay the price. I can hardly wait."

The oldest brother was surely the brains of the outfit, but I think even he was a little thrown off by my enthusiastic cooperation. Still, he managed to recover nicely and with a plan.

He barked instructions to the brother on the end. "Get behind him so he can't run away."

I smiled broadly. "I have no intention of running, kind sir."

The youngest brother did as directed and moved without caution. I caught him in the groin with a left side kick. He screamed in pain as he went down. The oldest moved next and I struck him in his dense belly fat with a right thrust kick, slowing him down enough to hit him in the face with my left hand. I swear the middle brother still had not moved. He watched as I followed up the left with a right cross that knocked his oldest brother to his knees. And then I began to walk toward him. I noticed his eyes alert to movement behind me. I ducked just as his younger brother hit him in the mouth. I landed an elbow on the nose of my attacker from the rear. The older brother had recovered and hit me with a good right hand right on my kisser. I felt the blood trickle down my chin and grinned.

I wiped the blood and looked at it on my hand as I smiled. "That's it. That is the best you got? Boy, are you in trouble."

I moved toward him with my hands by my side. His eyes told me that he wished that there were better odds to be had than three against one, though truthfully, I am not certain that you could count his brother who had dragged him into this little disturbance. He swung fearfully at my head with a blow that lacked purpose.

I ducked it easily and drove a hard left just above his kidney. He grunted loudly and leaned his body toward the pain he felt. I thought I would even him up so I dug a right into the same area on the opposite side. My blows were methodical and without anger. I smiled and said, "You can swing at the head all day but it does appear that a couple of good body shots sure does take the wind from a man, does it not?"

He gazed up at me and just for the absolute hell of it I grabbed the back of his head and kneed him under his chin. He collapsed in the sand. He was done. I turned to the other two. The middle one was still standing frozen with blood on his face from his brother's best punch of the skirmish. The little brother's nose was bleeding heavily. "Elbows are hard, aren't they? You boys care to converse some more?"

I received no response so I packed my stuff up and walked away, not even glancing back. They were done and I was feeling pretty good about everything till I heard the siren and glanced down the beach. The police SUV was about two hundred yards away and approaching rapidly. Two officers were standing on the Boardwalk watching me. It appeared that my options to escape were limited.

I stopped in front of the officers. I had seen these guys before. They were the same two officers that I watched yesterday, while I was hidden from their view in the woods. The older officer looked like a cop. He appeared to be a shade under six feet tall and a little overweight.

Maybe it was not that he looked like a cop but more that he carried himself like someone comfortable being one. He didn't strike me as someone who lived to abuse his power. And if he did there would at least have to be some kind of moral end to it.

I was certain that it was not the case with the younger officer. It wasn't his youth that belied his inexperience. It was his mannerisms. Every move was calculated and came off as being forced. There were scars on his face from a bad case of childhood acne. His head was shaved, but he was not bald. There was a dense mass of red stubbles of hair throughout. His compact build reminded me of a fire hydrant for some odd reason. I would bet my house that this guy abused his power anytime that he could get away with it. I am just as convinced that he waits until the odds are decidedly in his favor.

I looked at the older officer. "Do you mind if I put my stuff in my truck first, Officer? My license is in the glove box anyway."

He nodded and they walked on each side of me quietly to my truck. I put my stuff away, retrieved my driver's license, and turned toward them. I gave the older officer my license. "I guess you guys want to chat."

His partner whipped out his handcuffs enthusiastically. The older cop slapped his hand like he was a toddler. "Put those things away, Junior."

"But he just got in a fight and he matches the description of the guy that got in the fight yesterday at the restaurant."

The older officer rubbed his dark hair, looking at the rookie without warmth. His eyes returned to mine.

He and I both knew that the rookie screwed up any chance he had to catch me off guard with the events of yesterday. He also knew that I knew that he knew it was me. "Don't worry about the kid here. I wouldn't have been eased into some conversation where I admitted to something yesterday."

"Don't call me kid," Junior responded quickly with a high-pitched squeal that reminded me of Mike Tyson.

"Shut up, Junior," his partner stated evenly, without ever taking his eyes off me.

The slight ocean breeze changed directions just enough that the smell of donuts permeated the air. He noticed it as well. We both gazed in the direction of the smell. I bet we could have tracked down where the smell was coming from even if we didn't know where Britts was located, which we obviously both did. If I could not do it, I would wager that he could since he was surely a trained tracker of such aromas.

"Britts open today?" I asked. It was early in the season for them to be open during the week. They opened on the weekends in late March when people stood in line for hours that first Friday afternoon—regardless of the weather. They opened full time around Memorial Day for the summer. They made one donut, glazed. You watched the machine while they were turned out.

They are the best donuts I have ever eaten. Nothing else comes close.

"School's out today," he replied. "I guess they decided to open."

"How about I buy us a dozen, Officer Johns?" I said as I read the gold name plate pinned to his shirt.

"Will you throw in coffee also?" he asked, and I think he almost smiled. My charm should be what is against the law. Not beating up three rednecks. It probably is in some states.

"Wow. You broke me. Not only that I am going to confess to burning those buildings down. Just don't beat me with a rubber hose."

There had been a rash of vacant buildings burned down over the winter. We both gazed at the empty lot across the street where an old Motel once stood. It was one of the buildings that were a target of the arsonist.

I got the full smile this time. "Too bad we arrested that guy yesterday, and we don't use rubber hoses these days."

"Dang," I offered disappointedly.

We began walking toward Britts. The rookie began to speak and Officer Johns said, "Shut up, Junior," without breaking stride. He handed my license to him. "Go run this kid. We will be in Britts."

The kid joined us in record speed. Maybe he was afraid I might make a run for it, or the more likely scenario was that he was afraid he might miss out on the donuts.

The three of us sat for an hour and consumed a dozen donuts. Officer Johns and I talked about the development on the Island, baseball, and the invasion of tourist season that was just around the corner. The kid was not allowed to talk, though we did permit him to eat six of the donuts.

"I got the call yesterday for the restaurant. Do you know Ellie?"

I concealed a smile as I took a sip of coffee. He tried and he was smooth. I have to give him that. I scrounged my face up, though I hate to do that because it detracts from several of my best features. "What restaurant are you speaking of?"

"The one that is within walking distance of your house."

"I didn't even notice you look at my license. I better watch myself. You are a little too slick for my comfort. I might just be overmatched. Speaking of which," I added as I looked at Junior.

Junior eyed me with a puzzled expression.

"My DL?"

The perplexed countenance once again.

"May I please have my driver's license back?"

He laid it on the table and quickly consumed the remainder of his coffee.

"What about the restaurant?"

Officer Johns stared at me for nearly a minute,

waiting for me to say something meaningful. I know just how he feels as I've felt the same way myself at times. "Oh, the seafood place," I offered.

He waited for me to elaborate, which I had no intention of doing. The one thing people consistently do in a situation such as this is talk too much. Less is more. I knew better. The more you offer up the more you have to account for. I am not certain if I learned this from real life or from watching all those reruns of *Law and Order*. I loved Sam Waterston and Jerry Orbach. Jerry might just have been my equal in dispensing dry one-liners.

"I like Ellie," he offered. "Husband of hers isn't worth powdered shit. But something in her story did not ring true and it was hard to get anyone but the guy that got hit and his wife to give a description."

He waited for me to speak. I refrained. "Well, I guess we are done here. Thanks for the donuts and coffee," he said as he rose from the table. He adjusted his belt which contained the required cop accessories, over his protruding stomach. Donuts will do that to you. The rookie stood also and looked at his partner with a baffled expression. "You are not letting him go, are you?"

"What do you suggest that we arrest him for?" he asked tightly. His patience with Junior clearly strained.

"The fight on the beach," he retorted. His tone decidedly pitched again. "And we all know he hit that man at the restaurant yesterday."

Officer Johns looked at his partner with a bemused gaze. "Let me see if I understand. We arrest this guy for a one on three altercation with some of our most upstanding citizens? Why?"

There was no reply but I could see the deliberation process taking place between his ears. His eyes widened and he started to speak but he was interrupted again.

"I know Junior that we could take him to the station and have the couple come in and ID him."

"Yeah," Junior answered excitedly, thankful that his partner had put into words what he was too dense to verbalize.

"Not going to do that."

"But why? Because he bought us some donuts?"

"Well, there is that. I took a bribe and you ate half of them. Better keep this quiet," he added dryly.

Junior tugged at his shirt sleeves. The shirt he was wearing was about two sizes too small. I bet he spent half the day adjusting the sleeves to accentuate his thick arms. It reminded me of Bubba Skinner in the old cop show, *In the Heat of the* Night. A big difference though was I liked Bubba. He started to speak but was foiled yet again.

"Junior, even if the guy and his wife say it was him. Ellie is going to say it wasn't. I know her. She has her heels dug in pretty good about this and once she does that nothing is going to persuade her to do otherwise." He turned back to me as I stood.

"Have a nice day, Officer."

I got his stern look this time. "Be careful."

I nodded.

Junior excused himself to the restroom. Well, in his defense, he had consumed six cups of coffee. One for each donut, I surmised.

"Might be best to put Junior on decaf and maybe limit his sugar intake."

"That or a strait jacket," he replied deprecatingly.

"That was funny."

He extended his hand and I shook it. "I like Ellie. Anyone who defended her hasn't broken the law in my eyes."

"I am sure she is a nice woman."

He smiled broadly. "I don't recall when I have witnessed a man say so little and shovel so much BS at the same time."

"It's a gift," I replied with a beaming smile.

He turned and walked away. Junior emerged from the restroom, smirked at me, and then ran like a puppy afraid of being left behind to catch up with his partner. I don't blame him. Officer Johns would probably abscond without him if given half the chance.

§

I drove home and changed into exercise clothes. I had recently transformed the garage into a workout room. I jumped rope for five three-minute intervals with a minute rest in between.

Next, I began to hit the heavy bag that hung from the ceiling. My knuckles were sore so I wrapped them more heavily than usual before slipping my lightweight boxing gloves on. Just as I had with the rope, I did five three-minute rounds. The first round I stuck to a sequence of left jab, right cross, left hook, and right hook. After that, I punished the bag with a variety of blows in whatever manner suited me. Occasionally, I threw kicks in but with two surgically repaired knees, I generally take it easy on any snapping of my legs.

I wound down with a few minutes of hitting the speed bag. It sure isn't as easy as the professional boxers make it look. Still, after an awkward beginning, I was able to find a respectable rhythm.

I placed a mat on the floor and finished with ten sets of crunches and then stretched for a few minutes.

I bought the bag and assorted training items around the Holidays. I could just feel a rage building inside of me like a volcano just before it erupts. I thought the world might prove safer if I took my frustrations out by pounding on the heavy bag. I guess like a lot of things in my life that turned out to be a thwarted plan.

Still, the bags and the jump rope serve the purpose of getting a decent workout in during the days I don't feel like venturing into Wilmington to workout at the gym. There is something special about a day that I don't have to drive over the Snow's Cut Bridge, the high-rise bridge that leads you on and off the Island, that tends to be a better day all the way around. The bridge is also one huge advantage that Carolina Beach has over Wrightsville Beach, with its antiquated drawbridge that routinely backs traffic up for miles during the busy season. Some of their residents refer to the bridge as quaint. I could think of better words to describe it than that, but I feel I have used up my quota of curse words for the day.

I felt better when I finished. I walked to the fridge, retrieved a bottle of water, and drank it down quickly.

I showered for a long time, enjoying the hot water work my muscles over. I shut the water off and grabbed a towel. After drying myself I wrapped the towel around my waist and walked to the kitchen. I opened the fridge for another bottle of water. The fridge looked pretty slim. My staple of beer, eggs, and bagels is lacking. I dressed and drove across the street to the Food Lion.

I have lived on the Island now for a few years. It has proven a nice escape from Wilmington, which at times was quite stifling and an easy place to run into old girlfriends. My son encountered one of my former girl friends on the Boardwalk last summer. When he came home, he succinctly stated, "Dad, you can't swing a dead cat without running into one of your old girlfriends."

I guess the only way to screw this up is to get serious with a woman who resided on the Island. I did date one local woman for a brief period. Leigh was an attractive divorced mom with three young school kids and time was a luxury that she did not have. Most of our dates consisted of her meeting me at my doorstep around four in the afternoon as I was coming in from work. She would arrive clean and pretty but she would still get in the shower with me and in my bed a few minutes later. By five-thirty she left to go home to feed her kids. That was fine with me. I liked her but we both knew that it was not going anywhere. I also knew that she was using me to get her long term on and off boyfriend moving in the direction she desired him to. They had been split supposedly for a month when we met. But I knew they were still talking with each other. You just get a feel for these things. One day she quit showing up and I never asked why.

As I am wandering down the aisle at the grocery store debating if I need more than beer, bagels, and eggs, Leigh is coming around the corner. I can't begin to tell you how often I have thought of someone that I have not seen or thought about in a long time and turned the corner and boom they are there. Even though we resided on the same small Island we have not seen each other since one late afternoon when she left my bed for the last time.

She spotted me and immediate discomfort consumed her face. She looked good. She wore jeans with rips above each knee and a white top with a black blazer. The white top was very low cut and showed cleavage that was not present when we enjoyed our afternoon delights.

She also wore a wedding ring.

I gave my best half-assed smile. Did I mention that I have a variety of them? "Leigh, you look different. Did you change your hair?" I inquired as I gazed down at her chest.

She forced a smile that looked as if she had just stepped in something unpleasant. "Hello."

"You got married?" I phrased it as a question but it was not.

She looked down at her ring as if it just suddenly appeared. "Oh, yeah," she responded as she continued to look down.

Since it was apparent that she desired no part of a conversation with me—naturally, I pressed on. "To Sam, your old boyfriend, right?"

She nodded. "I need to go," she said tersely. "I have an appointment."

"It was nice seeing you," I cheerfully said, before adding, "Glad I could be of service." She pushed her cart away quickly. I grinned as I watched her walk away.

I sensed someone looking at me. It was Ellie. I waved. She ignored me and picked up her two bags of groceries and exited the store. I stood dumbfounded in the pet food aisle, which made absolutely no sense because I haven't had a dog in years. I kept waiting for Ellie to turn back. She doesn't.

Damn, doesn't anyone like me?

TUESDAY

It was ten o'clock in the morning, and I had not
punched, kicked, or even offered my sarcastic wit to
anyone. I was feeling pretty good about myself until I
realized that I had not yet ventured outside. Maybe as
long as no one made the mistake of knocking on my
door and antagonizing me the world was safe.

I deliberated about the brawl on the beach yesterday
and how truly easy it was even with the odds against me.
Curiously the entire fight seemed as if it all had taken
place in slow motion. The boxing work I did at home
probably aided my cause and there is little doubt that
I proved to be in slightly better physical condition than
my opponents.

But I know a better reason why I was triumphant
yesterday. I fear little, with the exception that my life
would grow lonelier as the years inched by. Micah would
never live in this area. The boy had New York City
written all over him from the beginning. He calls about
every other day but I have not seen him since Christmas.
I should be used to the empty nest syndrome but I am
not.

The first few weeks after I drove him to UNC-
Greensboro for his freshman year and left him alone in a
tiny dorm room; I immersed myself into home projects.
I built an entertainment stand for a large television that
was yet to be purchased. I painted three rooms. Two of
those required days of prep time because I decided to

remove wallpaper, chosen by the lady that owned the home previously. It was a bit feminine for a brawler like myself.

Mom, upon entering the house voiced her displeasure that I had removed the beautiful wallpaper. I didn't allow her comments to rile me and not just because I dearly loved her. It was more relevant that I think every woman alive considered herself an expert on interior decorating. The main bathroom in the house I grew up in had pink tile on the wall around the bathtub. The remainder of the wall had wallpaper with huge, gaudy flowers, and the dominant theme again was pink, with yellow and white the secondary colors. It might just have been the ugliest bathroom that I have ever witnessed. The half bath in the master bedroom also had pink tile on the wall complemented with a pink accordion door.

The ironic thing is that what the house did have were beautiful oak hardwood floors. So, what did she choose to do? She had the floors covered with an ugly pale green carpet.

I also removed the tiled counter with a painted fish sink that was in Micah's bathroom and replaced it with a white smooth countertop with the help of a co-worker who was more qualified than I in that area.

I purchased four tall oak bar stools and stationed them at the high counter that divided the kitchen from the living room. That way a woman could really admire me as I cooked dinner for her.

Micah was always with me, even for at least part of each week and that kept me grounded. During the period of shared custody with mother of the year, Tiffany—I never became accustomed to the solitude I felt after leaving him at her house.

It was a Sunday night, ironically one month before he would ask me to find a way for him to stay with me full time. I was driving home on River Road. The road was deserted that night, much like the desolateness of my soul. The emptiness swelled that night to such a degree that I began to weep. I see nothing wrong with a man shedding a tear and I have on many occasions. This was not that. This was a gut-wrenching sobbing that you might expect a small child to do when he watched the family dog being laid to rest.

That night it was as if all the lonely rides home morphed into one austere journey. I wept for the son I had to give back and the child that I never could give all my heart desired to.

My thoughts drifted to Officer Johns and how he knew but let me go. I also thought about the last part of our conversation. Ellie.

I don't know if it was loneliness that drove me to do what I did next or the need to do something else to fuel my already bizarre behavior of this week. I googled the number of the restaurant where the fun of this week had begun and punched in the numbers. I punch everything now that I am a fighter.

A woman with a nasal accent answered. "May I speak with Ellie please?" I asked politely.

"I'm sorry. She is off today. May I ask who is calling?"

"Yes ma'am. This is Roy at the brake shop across the bridge. She called yesterday and asked if there was any way we could inspect her brakes. Said they were squealing a bit."

"Well, try back tomorrow."

I caught her before she hung up. "That's a problem, ma'am. We are booked solid for the rest of the week. I hate to see something happen if those brakes are really bad. And on top of that, we have a pretty good chance of rain later in the week." Even I rolled my eyes at that last statement. I had no clue what the weather forecast was.

"Well, I am not supposed to give out home numbers of our employees," she answered quickly.

"I understand but I sure would feel better if I knew her brakes were safe." Too much or too little innocent charm I debated as I listen to her breathing as she contemplated the correct course of action.

"Oh, it can't hurt, can it?" She gave me the number. Just enough charm. I should have known better than to doubt.

I breathed deeply and called her.

"Hello."

"Ellie?"

"Yes, who is this?" she asked briskly.

"You would speak nicer to me if you only knew how

good looking I am."

"Listen jerk."

"I thought that your pet name for me was idiot and is that what you call someone who risked his very life all at the expense of your honor? And, might I add that I realize that you were just covering up your excitement at seeing me in the grocery store yesterday?"

She paused and laughed softly. Oh, I am an alluring devil.

"Billy, you idiot. How did you get my number?"

"I would just as soon you refrain from calling me an idiot."

"What do you want?" she asked impatiently before adding, "You said it was my pet name for you."

"We already have pet names for each other? Moving a little fast, don't you think?"

"So, what is my pet name?"

"Pumpkin?" I asked hesitantly. That was no good. The cunning woman had caught me off guard.

"Pumpkin?" she asked in disbelief. "That is the best you can do."

"I felt pressured."

"You pressured? Yeah, I believe that."

"Have you always been so cynical or is it just me that brings out this side of you?"

"What makes you believe you bring anything out in me?"

"Let's see, maybe the way you kissed me so forcibly.

I think you dishonored me. I might hang up and call an attorney. Unless…"

There was silence as I knew there would be. Ten seconds passed and then it grew to twenty. I was not going to cave. Who did she think she was dealing with? An amateur? Ten more passed. I made one mistake in this conversation. I would not make another.

"Unless what?"

"Have you had breakfast yet?"

"No, and what does that have to do with anything?"

"I thought I would cook breakfast for you."

"Suppose my husband is home."

"He's not. You would have hung up by now."

"You have a lot of nerve."

She had me there.

"You call married women a lot?"

I breathed in deeply. Where was I going with this? Now, it was actually me that did not know what to say. The seconds passed.

"Billy." Her voice softer.

"No, I don't. Forget it. I am sorry I bothered you. Bye."

"Don't go." There was a long silence that I saw no need to interrupt. "Will you really cook me a nice breakfast?"

"I will."

There was additional quiet. "Drive into the state park down to the river and then drive back slowly. I'll park in the lot at the end of the first left after you enter. I will walk the path to the edge of the main road and look for your truck at the edge of the trail. Make sure no one is on the road with you. See you in twenty minutes. Blink your headlights once." She hung up.

I did likewise and took a quick shower and put on blue jeans and a long sleeve teal shirt. It was time to leave.

I left home and drove to Carolina Beach State Park. It is a natural beautiful habitat. Two sides of it border the Cape Fear River and Snow's Cut Inlet, where the river makes its way to the sea. I passed an area that had several picnic tables and restrooms. As I reached the end of the road, where the marina was located, I surveyed the openness of the Cape Fear River. A huge cargo ship was slowly passing by heading in the direction of the State Ports.

Two older men were fishing on the bank. A middle-aged couple was easing their boat down off the boat ramp that is highly congested during the summer months. They both waved in my direction. I returned their waves. I wouldn't want anyone to think that I was not friendly.

I drove back in the direction from which I came. I slowed as I came around the curve and checked my rear-view mirror and then glanced in front of me; I am alone on the road.

I stopped directly across from the campground entrance to my left. Both campsites have looped roads and I often biked through the area. I looked at the trail to my right and saw no one. Maybe she had thought better about the idea but then she emerged from the trail that was bordered by a dense clump of small Turkey Oak trees.

She got inside my truck and we drove toward my house without a word. She had jeans on and a long sleeve tee shirt the color of butter and a black hat with the Nike swoosh symbol on it. Her blonde hair tucked under it.

We walked into the kitchen area and she looked around without comment. She took her cap off and placed it on the counter as she shook her hair free. She took my hand and I started to speak.

"Not one word," she said firmly as she placed a finger on my lips. Her hair was wet and smelled of apricots. I could smell body lotion that carried a hint of vanilla.

She led me down the hall to my bedroom as if she were the one who resided here. She stood over my bed contemplating about what was about to transpire. I watched her without expression. Whatever was filling her thoughts I knew she did not need or want to hear from me. For all my charm and bullshit, which may be one and the same this was a place I would typically be nice and say don't if you are not sure. And I would mean it. My mind went to another place, to the last woman that had been in this bed. I had hoped she was the last woman I would ever sleep with and we would sleep together a million times and then begin anew. I shook my head slightly as if I could clear the thoughts from it. She considered my expression. I forced a light smile.

"I'm not the only one thinking about someone else at this moment, huh?"

I shook my head tightly and refused to answer. She nodded as if she could understand my very thoughts as she moved toward me slowly. Her hands went to my shirt and slowly she pulled it over my head.

Later, after all movement ceased, she lay facing me, our bodies touching. I could hear our heartbeats beating opposite of each other. She shivered violently twice and then she fell asleep. I held her back with my hands and rubbed her slowly. Once she woke briefly and said, "That feels nice."

I wasn't sure I was allowed to speak yet so I continued to talk quietly with my hands. She fell asleep agan, and woke a few minutes later, smiled, and apologized. I rolled her over gently and we made love as if we were familiar lovers who had shared a bed for years.

She turned away and once again fell asleep quickly. I sure know how to keep a woman entertained. I kissed her shoulder a few times and laid there in the stillness of the morning. Birds were chirping quietly in the distance and I felt the first tranquil moment in quite some time. Oddly at that moment, I thought of a model train layout that Micah and I built years ago. The locomotive tried to replicate the sound of the horn a train produced. Have

you ever noticed how the horn of a train sounds different
at different times? In the daytime, the sound is neither
unique nor welcome. Micah and I once lived in a condo
in Wilmington. At just past ten every night I would hear
the horn in the distance as the train crossed Wrightsville
Avenue. The track was three miles away and the sound
proved both lonesome and comforting at the same time.
Many of those Sunday nights after returning Micah to
Tiffany—I sat in the room and watched the trains make
their way through the hills and woods and caves that we
had laid out together. I dreamed that such a place could
be real and that my son and I were escaping to a place
where we would never part.

I quietly rose and covered her up. I slipped black
gym shorts on and an old tee shirt and left the room—
closing the door gently behind me.

I went to the kitchen and put the coffee on. I got the
eggs out of the fridge, cracked them open, and stirred
them in a small glass bowl. I sliced some mushrooms
and shredded some pepper jack cheese. I sliced a potato
long and narrow for hash browns that I would sauté in
olive oil.

I was pouring a cup of coffee when she entered.
She was wearing my shirt. She reached for a cup and I
touched her hand. "I'll get it. Just sit there and watch my
talents go to work."

"I thought I already had witnessed that."

I think I might have blushed. She stood and reached

across the counter and touched my lips with her hand and winked. "Who said you could talk?"

There was a hint of sadness in her eyes, and I believe she witnessed the same in mine. There is no need to be dramatic. None of that tortured soul crap, but, in our eyes, we each saw life and the frequent disappointments suffered. Perhaps, what we had just done was wrong, but maybe it was worth it to escape from the frequent disenchantment that governed our lives.

"What was her name? The one that caused you to look off into the distance," she said as she offered a wink.

I smiled faintly. The woman she spoke of often winked at me and she did it slower and better than anyone else could. I did not want to think of her right now and the decision she made that left numbing heartache in its wake.

She nodded in understanding. "I'm not upset about it you know."

"I know."

She watched me cook as she drank two cups of coffee. I removed the chairs that were placed inverted on the table. We ate in silence with the exception of her proclaiming that the food was wonderful.

Later we cleaned up and she asked if she could borrow a toothbrush. I led her to the bathroom and removed a new one from the wrapper. We brushed our teeth in the double sinks like the couple we were not and never could be. I glanced in the mirror and studied her seductiveness.

"Why are you looking at me that way?"

"You are gorgeous."

"You don't need…"

I put my finger on her lips firmly. "Please don't make light of a compliment that I mean."

She nodded once and then she walked past me and touched my back lightly. What is it about the touch of a woman that makes the world outside and all its problems perish in that moment, if only for an instant?

"More coffee?" she asked as she walked with purpose to the kitchen. I followed her and sat on a bar stool and watched her make coffee. She looked across the counter at me with a question in her eyes that she was afraid to ask.

"Go ahead, Ellie."

"That is the first time you said my name since we got here."

"You kept shushing me. Now, what is your question?"

"Do I have to go?"

"What do you mean?"

She closed her eyes and shook her head in tiny shakes like I was the village idiot that failed to understand a woman. She had me there.

"Where is, uh?"

"Out of town working."

"And you want to stay how long?"

"I want to stay all day and all night. I want you to

take me to my car in the morning when the park opens. I want to be lazy with you and watch movies. I want you to go to the grocery store and get the items I need to cook dinner tonight." She had blurted it all out as if she were scared if she slowed down, she would lose her nerve.

"I would like nothing better."

"Thank you."

"For what?"

"For treating me like I am really something."

"You are really something."

There were tears in her eyes. And then she walked to me and held me for a long time. No one had to tell me that now was the time for silence.

We watched two movies that afternoon and then she cooked Eggplant parmesan for dinner with a beautiful salad on the side. I guess for all my adventures what I missed out on the most was someone special to cook for or with. To sit at a dinner table and enjoy a meal, a glass of wine and conversation. Dinner these days is spent with *Seinfeld* reruns.

We finished dinner and she asked what my favorite movie was. That was an easy one, *Tombstone*. We watched it together. It was probably the twentieth time for me and it was her first. She choked back tears when Wyatt Earp, (Kurt Russell) tracked down his love and told her that he had no money, no pride, no dignity but he would love her for the rest of her life.

The movie ended and I rose and walked to the DVD player. I ejected the movie and put it away.

"Where are the men like Kurt Russell in that movie? With that kind of heart," she added. When I failed to respond she asked, "Aren't you going to say that you are one of those men?"

"No. I was going to say that I was once."

The sorrow in my words startled me and it was as if an outsider had come into the room and spoken on my behalf. She eyed me curiously and then rose. "Let's go to bed."

"Thank you."

"For what?"

"For a really good day. For not eating alone. For not sleeping alone."

She was asleep so quickly. I admire people with that gift. It takes me a while each night to quiet the demons long enough to find rest. Dreams often come and go and rarely make any sense. It was as if a film was made with bits of my life all interwoven and out of order.

Sometime during the night; I woke as she snuggled in beside me and laid her head on my chest. I listen to her breathing become a slight snore. It was such a peaceful moment to be treasured in a life that has contained so little tranquility of late.

I've slept with maybe fifty women in my life and

I would have traded all of it for a million nights with one woman. One that could produce a feeling of contentment, somewhat like I felt at this moment.

WEDNESDAY

I woke to the sound of the shower. Moments later the shower shut off and I waited for Ellie to walk through the door. She was dressed in the same jeans and tee shirt. I guess she did not anticipate spending the night. Neither did I.

"Why did I do this?"

"It's okay."

She eyed me with a blank expression. It was not a question I was expected to answer. She sat on the side of the bed, refusing to look at me. I touched her leg, and she lightly smacked my hand. It reminded me of how Officer Johns had slapped Junior's hand when he attempted to handcuff me. I know my behavior can be seen as immature at times. Not that I am comparing myself to Junior in any way, shape, or form. I am pretty sure that I am a few steps higher than him on the maturity level. Not to mention brains, personality, and good looks, of which Junior has a face only a mother could love. Actually, it is not so much that I can be puerile as there are times that I tend to be a little too cute with my sarcasm. Either that or my audience just can't keep up. You decide.

She shook her head as if she were having a private dialogue with herself. There was something she wanted to say, more likely something she needed to say for her. I really didn't want to hear any explanation for what was the best day and night I have enjoyed since Mira walked away for reasons stated and unstated.

It must have been two minutes later when she began to talk. "I'm sorry. I knew what I was doing when I chose to come here. I am a big girl. Do you believe me when I say that I never did anything like this before?" The words she spoke were delivered with a heaviness that I would just as soon not deal with this morning.

"It doesn't matter. I am leaving him when he returns home Sunday." Her eyes studied mine for a reaction, for which I had none.

"And don't think you had anything to do with it," she added as if I had said something that gave her that idea. "This was in the cards a long time ago."

"Do you love him?"

She looked away and spoke as if she were in some remote place. Her voice was distant, barely above a whisper. "There was a time when he was such a gentleman, so kind, so thoughtful. We wanted to have kids but one of us had a problem. It eviscerated him. Once he was attractive, not that it was his looks that drew me to him in the first place. These days I count it a win if he showers. The passion he once had for me dissipated and now about the only thing that gets him excited is when there is a NASCAR race on television or even better when he can attend a race with his buddies.

I hate that crap."

I started to point out that I also hated NASCAR, but I held my tongue.

She turned back to me, smiled sadly, and laid her head on my chest. "You didn't sign on for any of this, did you? You just wanted to get laid."

I breathed in the aroma of her and knew it was at times like this a woman just wanted to be heard. There were several observations I could have made floating around in my busy mind, but I was wise enough to confine them all.

"I'm sorry. That was uncalled for. Despite your talent for fighting and clever remarks, you are a kind, sweet, and caring person. You made love with me as if I were someone really special," she said, her voice trailing off. "I have not been treated that way in far too long. Maybe one day there will be someone in my life that treats me that way once again and never stops."

I stroked her hair gently. Her remarks stung me slightly because there was no room for me in her scenario even though I was already privy to that information. I am the transition man. I thought about Mira and I wondered if that was all I was in her life. The first man she would stick her foot into the waters again with after she lost her husband. It was a far different transition than this. Someone had died and I could not compete with a ghost or guilt. They are worthy opponents that can't be defeated. It was hard to accept, but I wasn't left with much of a choice. Oh, I can comfort myself with thoughts of how it could have been worse. She could have said all that and I could have seen her on the arm of someone else the next week. That would have been worse but it still fails to help the sense of loss, and the pain that accompanies it.

"Tell me about her."

I merely shook my head.

"Did I hurt you by talking about a future with someone else? I'm in your bed and spent the night in your arms and yet I speak of leaving my husband and the day I am with someone else. It would be the way I would feel."

I smiled gently and replied, "Maybe just a little bit."

She rose and looked at me. "But you understand, right? We are both still in another place with someone else. They live in our hearts and the tender lovemaking we have enjoyed will be but a remote memory by the time we are ready to allow anyone inside of us again."

The poignant words were more than I cared to entertain this morning. "I am not up for this conversation."

She nodded with understanding. "I need to go soon. Take a shower and I'll cook breakfast for you."

I showered and put on workout clothes consisting of black compression shorts that were mostly covered by faded gray workout shorts and a black sleeveless stay dry shirt. We ate breakfast in silence and then I drove her to her car. Her red Camry sat alone in the parking lot where she had left it the day before. I sat in my truck with the engine idling waiting for her to get out. Not sure how to say goodbye. Not sure of anything right now.

"You got in another fight on the beach Monday," she said as she gazed at the woods in front of us.

"Ah, Officer Johns. My new best friend."

"He came back that night. To the restaurant," she added. "He knows it was you that hit that man last Sunday."

"I know."

"He knew I was dishonest about my description."

"I know that as well."

"Why did he let you go?"

"I protected you is how he sees it."

She looked back at me as if I had just told her I was taking a space shuttle to Mars the following week. "How do you know all of this?"

"Do you think I am just another pretty face and not wise and insightful?"

She refused to be dissuaded by my biting humor. "You are all of that. It is just that whatever has happened with you and the woman you still carry the torch for has somehow detached you from this world. It's really sad."

"Also, none of your business," I replied tersely. "I didn't ask for your dime store analogies."

She stared straight ahead and softly spoke. "Why is it that men think a woman will think less of them if they are vulnerable? God forbid they show a sign of weakness or have a tear escape occasionally?"

"Hey, you can save the Dr. Phil crap. The truth is women can say all that about wanting a man to be vulnerable, even weak at times. Women desire a man who has it together all the time. We can never break down or not be strong—in outward appearance if nothing else. The quickest way for a man to lose the respect of a woman is to allow weakness to come to the forefront."

"You really believe that?"

When I failed to respond—she charged ahead. "Maybe you just haven't found the right woman that you can be that way with."

"Perhaps."

"Are you strong all the time?"

"Only a fool would believe that, and I am not a fool in case you missed that." My last words ripe with condescension. I knew later I would feel terrible about that fact but at that moment my anger reigned over any other sentiment.

"Can I ask you something else?"

"Could I stop you?"

"Why did you hit that man in the restaurant?"

I shrugged.

"I can't hear your shoulders shrug?"

"Does it matter?"

"I think it does. Did you do it for me or did you do it for you?"

That is one of the many things about a woman. They

won't stop until they ask the really tough question. "I'm not sure."

"But you are sure about everything it seems."

I offered another shrug.

"Still can't hear that," she said tightly.

I shook my head. No shrug this time. Maybe that would stop her.

"When did you know that you were going to hit him?"

I had an answer for that one. "When he placed his filthy hand on me."

"I guess that is the answer."

"Look, you are far too bright for me. Whatever answers you think that you just received why don't you take them with you? You can pat yourself on the back as you leave."

She bit her lip and was quiet for a few moments, before responding, "You are right. You didn't ask for all this." She kissed me lightly on the side of my mouth as I refused to face her. She touched my face tenderly, but I was looking off into space dismissing her before she departed. She breathed deeply and then the door opened and closed. I heard her car start and drive away. I continued to look straight ahead into the woods. It was not one of my prouder moments. But then I have suffered a lifetime of those.

I shut the engine off and sat for several minutes. My eyes moved to the designated trail at the corner of the parking lot. It couldn't hurt to take a walk in the woods.

I walked easily down the trail, grateful that I was alone. For most of my life, Wrightsville Beach was the beach that I enjoyed. Perhaps that is why it seemed ironic that in a setting so close to the ocean there can be such an abundance of woods. The entire county was full of woods when I was a child. Now woods seem to be a rarity. Wilmington, our nice little quaint city was discovered. Land was clear cut for the plethora of neighborhoods that have been added in this area and there is no end in sight. Covid has fueled yet another huge growth spurt and now with land becoming scarce the contractors build higher and higher and our local politicians shrug and look the other way. No doubt the richer for it. I dreamed often of moving to a smaller undiscovered coastal area, but I am not sure such a place exists.

It was too early in the day to feel so utterly drained. There is lassitude inside of me that I can't escape. Why did I snap at Ellie? I could care less if the men I beat up this week lived or died, but the disappointment I feel will haunt me for—at the minimum—the remainder of the day. I know this about myself and I have known it for a long time, and yet I still don't understand it.

I heard a lady's voice calling the name Sparky. A spry Jack Russell came bounding toward me, dragging his leash without an owner attached to it.

"Whoa, Sparky," I said, as I knelt down on the

mulched trail. I scooped him up and was rewarded with a lick in the face. Maybe it was because I knew his name or it could be that my affluent appeal works on runaway dogs as well.

I heard a cry of desperation. "Sparky!"

"He is right here, ma'am. I've got him," I called out.

Moments later a slender lady with white hair and vivid hazel eyes rounded the corner. She was dressed in tan shorts and a white tee shirt that was mostly covered with a dark gray quarter zip windbreaker. The relief was imprinted upon her face. I thought she might be intimidated by my hulking self. She was not. She does not even seem to realize that I am a fighter. I think I may have to work on looking tougher. I don't want some little old lady getting the drop on me. Regardless of how sweet and innocent they may appear such as the one in front of me.

"Bless you, son. The little rascal got away from me." She took hold of the leash and I placed Sparky on the ground.

I nodded and smiled.

She laughed lightly. "I believe that he thinks he is a hunting dog. You know deer are quite prevalent in these woods."

"Yes, ma'am. I know. I ride my bike through here in the evening a lot. The deer are all over the place."

"You must live on the Island."

"Yes, ma'am. I live between the first two lights when

you cross the bridge. On the left."

"You are a well-mannered young man."

Well-mannered, maybe, young, not so much. Believe it or not, I have such a soft spot for sweet senior ladies that I kept my slick wit in check. "You can thank my mom for that," I said.

She nodded and was searching my eyes as if she were looking for an indication as to who I am. If she finds out maybe she will share that information. Lord knows I could use the help.

"She has passed away?"

"In most ways."

"You love her very much."

"And she I," I added as I looked beyond the scrub oaks to the towering pine trees off in the distance.

"Thank you for your help..."

"Billy."

"Mary."

I was wondering if we were supposed to shake hands at this point, but she did something I did not expect. She touched my face lightly. "I'll pray for you."

It reminded me of mom and something she would often say to someone who was facing the struggles of this life. My world has never been the same since her memory slipped away to an abandoned place no one could find. The tie that binds a southern boy to his mom is among life's most significant bonds. It was and is in my case the most influential. The loss of sitting on the porch, talking and laughing with her, and sometimes crying during the times it felt like she was the only person in the world who really loved me. The one person when everyone else turned away, including yourself, who still believed in you.

"Thank you, Mary." I petted Sparky one last time and walked away.

I reached a trail that looped back to the parking lot. The woods were quiet, save the sound of a woodpecker rhythmically tapping away at a decayed pine tree and I heard a boat motor off in the distance in the nearby river. Several feet ahead of me a black squirrel scampered across the trail.

I drove into Wilmington to work out at the fitness club that I had been a member of for several years. I spent forty-five minutes working out my upper body and another twenty minutes on the elliptical trainer. The gym was moderately populated for the time of morning. There was a group of married women, probably all in their thirties, who dressed sexily and had discreet tattoos peeking out from their spandex or in one case just above the right enhanced by plastic surgery, breast. One woman wore pink close-fitting sweats—the word PINK aptly written across her tight butt.

On the rare occasions, I was present when they were, I being the friendly person I am would speak to them in passing. They, having sold body and soul many years ago to the highest bidder, dismissed me without words.

One day I mentioned this to my friend Christopher, who worked at the gym as a personal trainer. He grinned mischievously and replied, "Oh, you mean the desperate housewives club."

An hour after my arrival I walked outside into the vivid sunshine. Working out certainly did not cure all my problems but it did allow light to seep into my grave mood. But on this day, it would fail to last.

§

11:10 P.M.

I knew that tonight was a night I needed to be home. The world would be safer and so would I. But my spirit was troubled—my thoughts too fragmented to refrain from harm's way. That is the only explanation for why I sat on a painted gray bar stool ordering yet another beer that I clearly don't need. It was the fourth bar I have visited on the Boardwalk and it is several rungs below the previous bars I patronized, which were quite nice. This one was dark, drab, and dirty—matching my temperament. I drove past this bar on Christmas Day, when it was open with maybe three or four lost souls drinking the holiday away. Tonight, there were maybe a couple of dozen desolate people present in this fine establishment, including me.

I had been unable to shake the disappointment of the morning parting with Ellie. Why did she ask about her? Why do women want to open your soul up so they can peek in? In my case, they would probably go running and screaming into the night if they could see in with any kind of precision. Not that I would blame them as I have felt that way myself on occasion.

A woman with a skinny face and huge brown hair with red highlights walked to the bar and stopped beside me. She wore a very short jean dress and shiny black boots that appeared to made out of plastic. Her legs were heavy and full of cellulite. Not exactly Tina Turner legs and definitely not the kind of legs for a dress this short.

The lady with the small face and large hair turned to me and offered the sexiest look she could muster. It fell as woefully short as a football kicker attempting a seventy-yard field goal when his maximum range was only forty yards. She wore a white top and her breasts were huge and hung low. Believe it or not, I sat impassively despite her allure. She looked away and turned back quickly, flipping her hair with her right hand as she did. The full-court press was on. She gazed at me and arched one eyebrow. Be still my beating heart.

"Buy a girl a drink?"

Was that a question or a statement? Not knowing I offered my D smile. No need to lead her on. "I'm sorry but if I did that you might want more."

Her face quickly was consumed in anger. "Screw you." And with that, she spun on her heels, pulled her skirt down, and waddled out the door. I think I heard the faint sound of thighs squishing in the distance.

The drunk on the bar stool next to me had watched all this with interest. By drunk, I mean a drunk worse than I, because I am still functioning at the moment, but give it time. He was smoking an unfiltered cigarette and he inhaled deeply and then blew smoke in my direction. Maybe he was agitated that she did not try enticing him with her feminine wiles. I made eye contact with the bartender. He looked at me and then at the gent smoking in a public bar, which thankfully there were laws against such behavior. He continued wiping the bar down, ignoring the violation. I guess the man was a steady customer.

I returned to looking at the man beside me. It appeared as if this would be one more dilemma that I will have to solve. He actually seemed in pretty decent shape for an obvious drunk. Genetics, it had to be. I couldn't see this guy ever exercising a day in his life. He looked oily like anything that hit him would slither off. He had thick coal black hair and eyes that nearly matched the color of his hair.

I raised one finger in front of him and said politely, "Blow that smoke in my direction one more time and I will knock your ass off that bar stool." My voice was low but sincere. Tough guys don't need to raise their voice.

His wobbly eyes fixated on mine. His face tightened and I knew that he was getting ready to offer a clever retort. "Listen..."

I looked around the bar. The clientele was scattered about in small groups. Two long-haired rednecks were arguing over a bet at the pool table. That seemed to garner everyone's attention at the moment. The drunk dragged on his cigarette heavily and blew smoke into my face. I hit him with a quick, short, right hand, and he collapsed off the stool to the floor below, which was appropriately as greasy as he appeared to be. Everyone turned toward us. I raised my hand to the bartender and motioned for another beer.

The two gentlemen playing pool walked over. One of them had a shaven, oversized head and a long ZZ Top beard. He was heavy and had to be at least 6'5". He wore jeans with a large set of keys clipped to a belt loop on his right side and a weathered black leather vest with a motorcycle emblem on the left. His pal was small and wiry with a severely receding hairline which made his stringy wheat colored hair that fell down his back look even more absurd. He was dressed in similar fashion to his cohort—minus the key chain. Both of them had arms inked with various designs of tattoos. I would wager that these guys have rebel flags mounted on their big four-wheel drive pickup trucks.

"What happened to Bernard?" The larger man inquired.

"One too many drinks, I guess," I replied with a slight shrug of my shoulders.

"He just fell off the stool is what you are telling us?"

"Draw your own conclusions. All I can tell you is he was sitting on the stool one moment and the next he was on the floor. I think it is what you might refer to as a mystery."

"I think that you are a liar, and I don't believe you."

"That is a bit redundant, don't you think?"

Their brains were now at full throttle. I thought I smelt a smell similar to wires burning but I couldn't be positive. I thought I would help these fine gentlemen with the idiosyncrasies of the English language.

I spoke very slowly. "Redundant." Still, they did not grasp it. Ah, God bless the ignorant redneck.

"You said I was a liar. Well, it is redundant to add that you don't believe me. Repetitious," I added. They might get that one. But judging from their blank expressions, perhaps not.

What is strange about all of this is that while I was dispensing the obviously much needed English language lesson to Bubba and Elroy, not one person has been concerned enough to check on Bernard. I don't think it is my place to do so since I am responsible for his being there. So far, Bernard had not stirred from his slumber to share his version. I don't really know if the men in front of me are named Bubba and Elroy but it does seem to fit. Bubba being the larger of the two men.

And at that moment when you think life can't even remotely become more entertaining the heavy oak door swings open and in walked a young, obviously out of place interracial couple. They were holding hands. Don't ask me why but for some strange reason I have an inkling that my newfound pals Bubba and Elroy are not going to like this.

They are a very attractive couple—not Bubba and Elroy but the couple who just entered. He is a small, very handsome black man. His features are smooth and he could probably make a career modeling if he were inclined. He reminded me of a younger Taye Diggs. His companion is a tall blonde, and though she has on jeans and a cream-colored sweater I bet she has the legs to wear short skirts if she were so inclined, unlike my earlier companion. She wore spiked heels that added four inches to her height. How in the world do women walk in those things?

They are as out of place as I would be at a black-tie dinner at the local country club. They walked toward the bar and almost stepped on Bernard. They looked at each other and began to retrace their steps but the two gentlemen that I have been conversing with blocked their path.

The smaller man put his hand on the lady's chest to stop her or to cop a cheap feel. I am not sure of which. She shoved him back hard with both hands. "Get your hands off of me!" she shouted.

The larger man looked down at her boyfriend and back to the lady. "What is the matter? You couldn't get a white man?"

Since I abhor racists and I have been spoiling for a fight since I walked into the Boardwalk area there seemed to be only one course of action. "Thank you, God," I silently whispered. I rose slowly and grabbed the smaller man by the back of his neck and slammed his head down onto the bar as hard as I could. Blood splattered in several directions including the bartender's face and then Elroy slumped to the floor, falling unconsciously right on top of Bernard. Bubba caught me with the end of his pool stick in my gut. I backed away and tried to catch my breath. It wasn't easy. He kept coming toward me, brandishing his pool cue like a baseball bat. He swung hard enough to have sent my head into the Atlantic. I ducked just in time and felt the breeze from it as it passed. I mustered all the strength I could find and I hit him low on his right side. He staggered back and regrouped. The intensity of the anger in his face should have concerned me but it did not. What's the worst that could happen here? Whatever it is I really don't care.

The remainder of the crowd observed intently but thankfully no one joined in. I am pretty certain I don't have any supporters. The couple was frozen in place. The smart thing for them to do was to get the hell out of this dump, but they had not chosen that route.

Bubba came at me again, slower this time, more calculating. I couldn't count on a wild swing at my head this time. I tried to straighten up but the pain in my stomach would not fully allow it. The moment he started to swing he screamed as he grabbed his knee. The lady had kicked him hard on the back of it. I guess those four-inch heels are more than a fashion accessory. He turned with ferocity toward her and regardless of whether I could breathe he was not going to hit a woman in my presence. I mustered everything I had and ran as hard as I could and tackled him just above the waist and drove him on top of one of the tables with such a fury that Lawrence Taylor in his prime with the Giants would have been proud. Bottles and beer mugs from the table slid off onto the floor along with us. Broken glass was everywhere. He was moaning now and I rolled off of him to the grimy concrete floor. He was done and it was a good thing. I am pretty sure that I am spent as well.

She knelt by me. "Thank you," she said.

I noticed the sirens wailing in the distance. "Why don't you and your friend get out of here?"

"No," he said. "The cops will be here and we need to tell them what happened."

"Just go. I don't need your help."

She shook her head slightly. "We had no business in this place. We heard the stories but we had a few drinks at the Marriot and I just had to come here. The one bar we were warned specifically to stay away from. It was my stupid idea and my fault and now you are hurt and the police are coming." She was rubbing my face lightly as she spoke. What is up with everyone touching my face?

"Where do you guys live?"

"Maryland," she answered.

"Would you help me up?"

"Are you sure?" he asked.

"Look at this floor and ask me that again. Hurry before I catch something." Each of them got on the opposite side of me and helped me up. I managed to sit in a chair at an adjacent table where I could keep an eye on Bubba. He had managed to sit up but that was as far as he had gotten.

I felt my mid-section and speculated as to the extent of my injury. It sure hurt like hell. They each pulled up a chair and sat with me at the tattered table.

"My name is Holly and this is William."

"Billy," I replied. "It's nice to meet you. Rather strange circumstances but what the heck," I said, with a slight shrug of my shoulders.

She smiled softly. "Why did you help us?"

"Besides the fact that I hate bigots?"

She chuckled. "Yes, besides that."

"How about if I just wanted to hit someone?"

She studied my face and found nothing to reassure her that I was joking. "And my being with a black man doesn't bother you?"

"Are you conducting some kind of social experiment?"

"No."

William smiled and said softly but with conviction. "She always has to have the answers."

"Does it?" she asked, undeterred.

"Should it?"

She didn't answer.

"Do you love him?"

She smiled and her entire face lit up. "Very much so. He is just not much of a fighter." She laughed softly.

"There are far more important things than that."

"Thank God," he said sarcastically.

"I bet you are really smart though."

She answered for him. "Valedictorian of his class in high school and a 3.8 GPA at Yale."

I love it when a woman speaks for her man in a loyal proud way. It must be quite a feeling.

"Can I get you anything?" he asked.

"Pacifico. Thanks."

He gave it to me just as the police arrived. I smiled at the lone officer as he stood in front of me with a look of boredom.

"Officer Johns, what a pleasant surprise. Night shift so soon?" I drank heartily from the cold beer.

"I switched shifts with someone being the sweetheart of a guy that I am. His daughter was sick."

He looked around at the regulars including the three on the floor that were sitting on the floor in a daze. He pulled a chair out and sat. "What happened?"

The bartender spoke first. "That son of a bitch comes in my place and wrecks it. I never even seen him before and then he turns all Rosa Parks on these guys when she brings that colored man in here."

Despite pain that made it difficult for me to breathe properly, I began to giggle, and then it built into uncontrollable laughter. I looked at William. "Colored. He called you colored. We have been transported back in time. It must be 1965."

And then I be damned if William did not begin to snicker and his girlfriend joined in our laughter. I could tell Officer Johns wanted to take part but he was intent on being professional. He removed his hat wearily. "Fred, shut up until I ask you something. And how could anyone wreck this place?" he added despairingly, motioning with his hand as he looked around the dimly lit bar.

Holly spoke up. "I will tell you what happened."

He gestured for her to begin.

He listened to her version, which was pretty accurate. He turned to William, who merely nodded.

He rose and looked at the three battered men who were now sitting on bar stools. He zeroed in on Bernard. "How did you get on the floor?"

"He hit me," he answered, pointing at me.

"Can you prove it?"

It took him a long time to find a voice. "Prove it?" he asked. The thought had obviously never occurred to him.

Officer Johns turned back to me. "Did you knock him off the stool?"

I smiled with all the insincerity I could muster and said nothing.

He rolled his eyes. "Okay, here is what is going to happen. No one is going to jail and no one is driving home. I assume that is okay with everyone." He didn't wait for an answer as he looked at William and Holly. "Walk very quickly to the Marriot and do not come here again."

"We learned our lesson," Holly said. She rose and then kissed me on the cheek.

William placed his hand on my shoulder and said, "Thank you." They departed back to the safety of the Marriot.

Officer Johns shook his head, feigning disgust. "Everybody's hero, huh?"

"Even yours?" I chimed in with feigned innocence.

He shook his head in slow weary shakes. "Not mine."

He rose from the table. "C'mon, let's go."

"I know about you Carolina Beach cops. Will they ever find my body?"

"Will anyone care?" he asked dryly.

Not even I had a quick retort to that.

"I am escorting you home. You can't drive in this condition, and I don't want the boys in here to get brave after I leave."

I rose gingerly. "You sure you aren't better suited to be a nun rather than a police officer?"

"I grew up Catholic. Trust me. Nuns are not close to

being as sweet as I am."

We walked to his patrol car, and he retrieved a kit from inside. "Lift your shirt," he said.

I did as I was told and I am sure I threw him off when I did it without a remark. Not exactly a continuing history in my life. Sometimes even I need a break from my acerbic wit. He felt around in the damaged area. "Nothing broke but you might want to get it looked at."

I nodded.

He shook one of those instant ice packs and popped it. "Put this on it and get in."

"Front seat or back?"

"Get up front now," he barked.

"I would prefer to ride in the back. Get the full chauffeur thing, you know?"

He glared and pointed to the front.

"As you wish."

He gave me the tough cop glare and I, frightened beyond reason quickly got in the front seat.

"You ever watch that show *Third Watch* that was on television several years ago?"

"You ever think that I live this stuff and therefore have no need to watch a show with cops in it when I get home?" he remarked as he drove out of the parking lot.

"Well, if you haven't watched it how do you know there are cops in it?"

He glared at me once again with that frozen cop look that is designed to make me shiver in fear.

"If you do that again, I might wet myself."

"Do what?"

I gave him my best imitation of the tough guy cop look.

He laughed and shook his head. "Damn," he muttered and exhaled deeply.

"Don't worry about it, Officer. I'm like that. I grow on people. It just takes time. It's kind of like your first beer. You don't like it initially but..."

"So, you're an acquired taste?" he interrupted.

"Yeah, that pretty much sums it up."

"I still don't like you," he said with his tough guy voice and stern facial expression. The combination was almost lethal.

"Yes, you do," I replied. "You couldn't help it even if you tried."

"I am trying," he responded.

"But without success," I replied quickly.

He muttered something undecipherable. He changed the course of the conversation since he could not compete. "Why did you mention *Third Watch?*"

"The cop on there, Sullivan. You look like him."

"He is a lot heavier than me."

"Maybe by a dozen donuts."

He glared at me. I smiled broadly. "He is my favorite character."

"The show streams on Tubi now."

I paused for a few moments before adding, "You sure

know a lot about a show that you never watched."

"My wife binge watched it last year. She said Sully looks like me but that he is much heavier and not as good looking."

I nodded and shrugged at the same time. "I'm sure she is right," I said without conviction.

He eyed me with a slightly puzzled expression.

I nodded, without the shrug this time. "Of course, she is right."

He shook his head wearily.

He stopped at the light. I pointed to the convenience store to our right. "I am out of beer. I don't suppose you might want to stop so I can purchase a twelve pack do you?"

The look he gave me pretty much confirmed that he would not care to accommodate my request. Actually, I am just pulling his chain. There is beer in the fridge at home.

Minutes later we were parked in my drive. The car was idling and neither of us spoke. He seemed troubled and uncertain of what to say so I thought I would help him out. It is just part of my giving nature to come to the aid of my fellow man.

"I ain't asking you in for a nightcap, Officer and I ain't kissing you good night either," I added for good measure.

He did not even crack a smile. It appears the man has no sense of humor.

"Why did you go in that place? I never saw you there before. I know all the regulars. You are a step above the rift raft that hangs out there. Are you spoiling for trouble? Do you have a death wish or something?

"I ran your records. All that is on it is a marijuana conviction when you were eighteen and three speeding tickets. What gives?"

"Nothing gives, Officer Johns."

"Yeah, a fricking *meltdown* by a forty-eight-year-old man. Three fights in four days."

I opened the door and walked in front of the car. "Thank you," I said, but he was already backing out of the drive.

That is two exits today where I left people pissed off. Oh well, there is always tomorrow.

Thursday

It was one o'clock in the morning, and I've been in the shower for thirty minutes trying to wash the festivities of the night away. I turned the shower off and reached for a towel. My phone rang. As bizarre as this week has proven I don't even find it out of the ordinary that I have a phone call at this peculiar time of morning. I wrapped the towel around me and the excess water fell to the tile below and I slipped slightly and almost busted my naked ass before recovering with the grace of a figure skater.

I make it to the phone. "Hello."

"Did I wake you, Dad?"

The very resonance of my son's voice warmed me. "I was awake. I have been down at the Boardwalk getting into fights."

There was silence where I expected a slight laugh at what he surely will believe to be a joke. He has something on his mind. I wait. Silence is a great tool in raising children. Parents want to fix everything—bark instructions. Children want to be heard. I waited a little longer. I have nowhere to go and even if I did, I would stay right here till he received whatever assurance it is that he needs.

"I had a bad feeling, Dad. Actually, a bad dream, and I wanted to see if you were okay."

We have always had that kind of connection. The distance between us has not touched that. My mind wandered to early mornings when he was little. How I missed waking up with a small child already awake, munching on dry cereal, and watching cartoons.

Many people complimented me about how well I raised him but truthfully, I made many mistakes. He was a low maintenance child and even better, forgiving of my numerous parenting miscues. I never felt like I did enough for him and he always thought I went beyond what he had the right to ask for.

"Dad, are you there?"

"Yes. Tell me about the dream."

"You were in the middle of this large room and all these people surrounded you. I didn't recognize anyone but you. Everyone was angry and they were closing in. They had bar stools, sticks, and various weapons to beat you with. It was a mob. It was so vivid."

"Micah, I am okay. The week has been crazy. I won't lie to you about that."

"Dad," he interrupted. "You have never lied to me about anything. I could always go to you and get the truth even when it was not what I wanted to hear."

I breathed in deeply the love my son's words contained. "Tell me what is going on with you. Any bites on any parts?"

He was silent for a few moments and I knew he was troubled about more than me. "I'm chasing my tail, Dad," he offered wearily.

"You are not giving up on your dreams. It will happen if you don't give up."

"I'm behind on my rent. I got fired from my job because I was a few minutes late because an audition ran over."

"Listen to me. You get off your ass first thing in the morning and find another job. New York City is a pretty big place."

"But Dad, maybe..."

"Maybe, my ass," I interrupted. "How much money do you need to tide you over?"

"You raised me to stand on my own two feet."

"You can pay me back when you hit it big. I tell you what. You can pay to take us to Alaska for a two-week trip and we will call it even."

He chuckled softly. "That is a deal. We will do it—just you and me."

"I did okay with the sale of my business. I don't want you to worry. I'll wire ten thousand to your account first thing in the morning."

"Too..."

I interrupted him. "Just be smart with it and don't argue with me. I am your dad, and I will do as I please."

"Dad, please don't interrupt." I didn't. "You are not only my dad. You are my best friend."

What does a man say to that? Even I know when to say nothing and savor the words, this poignant moment.

"Dad, are you there?"

"You ordered me not to interrupt."

"Dad, no one has ever ordered you to do anything."

We laughed softly together.

"Now tell me what else is going on."

"There is a school here that a big director told me that I would be well served to attend. He likes my work but he thinks I need more refinement of my skills."

"How much does it cost?"

He breathed deeply and then laughed loudly. "Oh, about twenty-five grand a semester ought to take care of it."

"We don't have to solve everything right now. Let's take it step by step. Pay your rent. Credit ratings are important but not as important as your word. You pay your bills like I taught you. Never sell your word. Never cheapen it."

"I won't. Thank you."

"Don't thank me till you get my bar tab from our big trip," I said with a chuckle.

His laughter was freer this time. He began to talk and the familiar animation that has been present since he could talk was back in his words. "The director that likes my work thinks I do sad emotions better than nearly anyone my age."

I nod even though he can't see me. "How do you do it?"

"Well Dad, each time I need to cry or be afraid I just recall you and me in my dorm room. Seventeen years old and wanting so badly for you to take me back home and the two of us hugging each other and you encouraging me as we both sobbed."

"Yeah," I whispered.

"You were crying so hard at the end you could only tell me two things. Remember, Dad?"

"I do."

He proceeded anyway. "You said, 'I love being your daddy, and you are the greatest thing that has ever happened in my life."

There was silence again as I waited for him to continue. "I love you, Dad."

"I love you."

"Bye."

"Never doubt your ability to make this happen, because I don't."

"I won't. Thanks."

"For what, a few bucks?"

"No, not just for the money but for always believing in me. Bye, Dad."

I tossed the phone on the bed. I would not be involved in altercations if he were still here. He kept me grounded.

I put jeans on, an old nearly faded to white denim shirt, and black Reebok cross trainer shoes. I don't think I will sleep tonight. My mind was racing at Mach one speed. It would probably blow up one day. Too many rapid-fire thoughts at one time. Maybe they could engrave that on my tombstone. *One thought too many... and boom!*

I walked into the kitchen and retrieved a Pacifico from the fridge. As if I had not consumed enough alcohol. My thoughts lingered on my son. There was no way I could pay for the school, not alive anyway.

I have a 401K and a nice chunk of equity in my house. Five years ago, I took out a life insurance policy for $500,000. But what I have in liquid assets won't even touch the money he would need to go to school. It occurred to me just like it did Jimmy Stewart in *It's a Wonderful Life* that I am worth more dead than alive.

I thought of Ellie and Officer Johns. I did not want either of them to be angry with me. I rose and took a step toward the garage when I realized my truck was not there. It was in a parking lot adjacent to the Boardwalk. I debated about walking to retrieve it but if Officer Johns were still on duty that would really piss him off. Besides, he strikes me as a decent guy. I've disappointed him enough tonight and at this moment for some strange reason that matters in a week that I scarcely give a rat's ass about anything.

A feeling of lonesomeness engulfs me. I think of mom and the last years of her life being spent suffering from dementia. During her more lucid moments, she praised her God for being so kind, so wonderful, and so loving. I spend these days cursing him for allowing her to suffer. Maybe in between the two of us lies the God he really is. Truthfully, I don't know.

Mom was always there to love me when no one else could. I sighed deeply. Tonight, I missed her more than ever.

She always stood by me. Even during the times, she did not understand me. She watched me pursue dreams that never came to fruition until dementia robbed her mind. Never did she give up believing that I would find my way. I can hear her now saying, "A heart as big as all outdoors and a mind that seldom knows a moment of peace." She would say that with a tired smile, laced in sorrow because she wanted to find a way to grant me what my heart desired. If it were in her power, I would have had all my dreams come true a long time ago. I would be living the fairy tale. But fairy tales only exist in storybooks.

My thoughts drifted to Ellie and I closed the door behind me and began walking toward her house. She told me she lived on St. Joseph Street and I recognized where when she told me. As a boy, my great Aunt Ada lived on that street in a house that remains standing today. The home is probably eighty years old and it rests on land that touches the waterway. I would have thought someone would have bought the house and demolished it by now. That is the wave of Carolina Beach. The land is worth so much more than a house that people lived and raised families in.

Standing slightly offset in front of the old house is a detached garage that her husband Thomas built. He built it out of lumber that washed up in their yard from the great Hurricane Hazel that battered the east coast in the fall of 1954. I was not here to see that one but the old timers, including dad, talked about it as if it occurred yesterday. It was the storm in this area that proved the measuring stick for all the storms that followed.

Twenty minutes later I was in the drive of a small cottage that rested on the ground. Ellie's car was parked near the house. It was across the street from the water and wetlands bordered it on each side.

I walked to the back of the house and saw a glimmer of light in what I assumed was the bedroom. I tapped on the window. She rose, walked to the window, and moved the curtain to one side. She studied me as I offered my best smile and cocked my eyes at her. She probably could not see clearly in the darkness, but it couldn't hurt, could it? She looked at me without expression. Maybe she was hoping I would go away. I had not lost a fight all week and I was not about to lose this one. I stood there stubbornly and I even deprived her of my smile. That will show her.

She broke as I knew she would and pointed to the back. I met her at the back door where she continued to look at me without expression or words.

"Probably be better if you let me in before someone sees me."

She remained frozen in place.

"I'm not leaving and you aren't calling the cops so..."

She deliberated a little longer. Finally, she opened the door. "Come in before someone sees you."

Didn't I just say that? I entered quickly and she closed the door behind me. "Excuse me if I don't turn the lights on. The curtains are not exactly made of premier fabric."

She led me to the kitchen and retrieved a bottle of water for each of us. She motioned to the dark gray metal kitchen table and I sat in a metal chair that did not match. Probably best to keep that observation to myself.

I looked at the bottle of water and said, "I was hoping for something a little stronger."

"I doubt that you need anything stronger," she

answered deliberately.

"Sorry if I scared you."

"Thought it might be you but I had my pistol just in case."

We sat in silence before she said, "You woke me to do what? Sit here and say nothing."

"I thought maybe you were lying in bed thinking of me."

She stared and did not bat an eye. There was anger in her eyes but behind the ire, there was sorrow that governed those deep brown eyes.

It was plain even to me that my charm, or bullshit, I get confused over which is which, was not going to suffice at the current moment. Well, there is always the truth for one to fall back on.

"I'm sorry for the way I did things this morning. I was thoughtless about your feelings."

"You were that."

"I was that."

There was quiet as she studied me. "That's it. No witty remarks or observations."

"Just one."

She gestured with her hand for me to continue. I did.

"Why is it that when it is dark and you can't fit the key in the door to your house that you always have to pee?"

She studied me for several moments and then replied

evenly, "Maybe it is because the fact that you have to pee diminishes your ability to fit the key in the door."

I shook my head in utter disbelief at her perceptive analogy. "I never thought of that," I responded, dumbfounded that this particular scenario had escaped me all these years.

I took her hand across the table and I felt her try to resist but she left her hand in mine and tickled the back of my hand slightly with a finger. Maybe for once it is not my irrefutable charm but her solitude and need as well.

"I am sorry for my ugly behavior. I am a better person than that, believe it or not."

She nodded. "I believe it."

"Thank you. You are kinder than I deserve under the circumstances."

"You're welcome," she whispered, her words steeped in sorrow.

I rose to leave. I walked to the door and placed my hand on the doorknob.

"Try not to be so hard on yourself. You're a good man. You have just had some hard blows and lost your way."

I nodded once gently.

"And I am not trying to be Dr. Phil," she quickly added.

I closed my eyes for a moment. "I know."

"Besides, I am a lot cuter than he is."

"You are way more than cute. You are a beautiful woman. One day when you are ready, I will envy the man that gets to lie down with you and wake each morning looking into your eyes."

She shook her head in slight disbelief. "What does a woman say to something like that?"

"Probably nothing."

"That is the most wonderful thing anyone has ever said to me."

"I said you were supposed to say nothing."

Light entered her eyes as she smiled.

"Where is your truck?"

"It's at the Boardwalk. Officer Johns gave me a ride home." I turned the knob and opened the door.

"Did he give you a ride home because you drank too much?'

"Yes," I answered, pausing, without turning around. I stood staring out into the woods behind her house. I waited to see if there was more that she wanted to say. Silence engulfed us.

"I'm truly sorry, Ellie." I pushed the door open, stepped outside, and turned to close it—offering her a slight smile.

"I'm lonely," she said.

I stepped back inside and closed the door slowly. She rose and placed my hand in hers and led me to her bedroom.

The moonlight was streaming through the window.

I saw her eyes rest on the bruise that had formed from my earlier encounter. She looked into my eyes and shook her head in tiny shakes. She touched my bruise gently. "Why, Honey?"

"Honey," I repeated.

"Sorry," she said.

"Don't be. Say it again."

"Honey," she repeated as she knelt down and delicately kissed the bruised area. She lifted her head, looked in my eyes. "You desire a life where you walked in the door at the end of the day and someone called you honey, and her eyes sparkled at the sight of you. Big tough guy like you."

"As bad as it pains me to admit, I may not be all that tough."

"I knew that already, but I promise not to let your secret out," she said softly, wearing an ever so slight and seductive smile.

We were quiet as we lay in bed. Somewhere in the distance, I heard the sound of a large vessel moving on the waterway. My mind slowed to a place not so sinister.

I woke as the first faint light from the false dawn filtered into the bedroom. She stirred and then rose. I heard the toilet flush and the sound of her brushing her teeth. I drifted off again and when I woke, she was sitting beside me at the edge of the bed.

I thought of my son and something inside of me felt as if I might never see him again. I shuddered as she pressed her warmth down on me.

"Honey," she said.

I closed my eyes and drank in the warmth of her voice. Maybe it was our need, our desolation, perhaps our desperation, but I felt love. It was not the powerful love that I have known, but it was soothing and earnest and we clung to it in our despair.

She rose and returned minutes later. Opening a container of Blue Emu, she scooped some out, rubbed it between both hands and then gently applied the ointment on my latest bruise with a compassion that had been sadly absent in my world. I started to speak and she softly said, "No. Let us have this moment. This place in time of tenderness that nothing will ever be able to pry away."

She finished doctoring me and placed the container on a wooden apple crate that was turned upside down, serving as a nightstand. There was faded writing on it from a black sharpie. Phipps Apple Orchard, Woolwine, Virginia. The two of us laid on our backs. I felt her take my hand into hers and then she fell asleep. I listened to her breathe in the stillness of the new day breaking. I knew it was time to depart, though it was the last thing that I desired to do. There was a feeling of closeness, of intimacy, in this small bedroom that I wanted to keep, but it and she do not belong to me.

The light from the sun grew stronger. I rose and dressed and then kissed her gently, covering her up as

I did. She looked content. I am certain that she too has known little peace in her life. I know that since she is married what I am doing is wrong, but I refused to feel immoral. God probably disagrees but I reached a point where I no longer cared what he thought. It is only at times such as this that I'm glad mom is not able to hear me ever say that. I'm also grateful that she does not know that I have not set foot in a church since the day we admitted her to that facility.

I walked out the back door and continued south through the woods. It was difficult to find dry enough land to walk on without sinking in mud, but the farther away from the road I walked the wetlands grew firmer. I forged my own path as I have throughout my life. Mom often said God had a path just for me. If that were accurate, I never saw the roadmap.

I made my way to the road that ran behind Cinema 4. I thought of Micah and the years he worked there. The movies we went to see together and how important he felt that he could get me in for free. It helped to know people in big positions like running the box office at the movie theatre.

I was almost to the main highway when a late model, white Ford 150 truck stopped beside me. "Get in," Officer Johns instructed.

"What are you doing up so early?"

"I just got off an hour ago. Believe it or not, you are not the only troublemaker on the Island. We had three domestic disputes after two o'clock. The last call the woman had used a butcher knife on her husband." He shook his head. "It was not a pretty sight."

"The knife wound or the wife?"

"Neither," he replied with a grin. "Come on. I will give you a ride."

We rode in silence to my truck. He stopped and shut the engine off. "Coming from Ellie's." It was not a question.

I started to open the door and his big hand latched on to my arm. The sudden movement caused me to wince in pain.

"Sorry."

I breathed deeply. "It's okay. Thanks for the ride."

"Wait a minute. I'm off duty. Let's just talk. Forget that I am a cop."

I took my hand from the door and looked straight ahead.

"I know that you view yourself as some kind of intuitive genius."

"Intuitive," I turned to him with a mock expression.

"Think you are the only one that knows a few fancy words?"

We were silent for a while and then I asked, "Why? Why this interest in me? Surely you have better things to do with your life than nursemaid some meltdown."

"First off, Bubba. I ain't your nurse. Second, your old man was a cop once."

I looked at him as if he had just said he lived with wolves as a child. "Yeah, my old man was a cop and he called me Bubba. I suggest you not follow down that path."

He raised his hands in retreat.

"What else do you know, Dick Tracy?"

"You have a son in New York City and I think it would be a grand time to visit him. I have a bad feeling that if you stick around here one of us is going to regret it or both."

"I got the same feeling. I had it ever since I slugged that idiot in the restaurant Sunday."

"You just slipped up and confessed." He was grinning broadly.

"No, I did not. I told you what you already knew. But you won't do anything about it."

His expression asked why.

"You asked if we could talk and to forget that you are a cop. And you also know the jerk got what was coming to him. A man like you has values that don't lock him into following a book some guy with a master's degree that never walked a beat wrote. You follow what you think best, and in the process, you are a better officer than the one that goes strictly by the book. And," I paused for effect. "It would also mean that Ellie lied to an officer and you won't go there because there is a reason you take such an interest in her. She is important to you but I don't know why."

He looked away and began to speak in a voice so small it reminded me of hushed conversations in church. "Her dad was a cop, and I was his partner. He taught me most of what I know about being a cop. His name was Henry. He was caught alone one night off the Boardwalk by some bad guys that he had several run-ins with."

He placed his hands on the steering wheel. He was gripping more than the black wheel as he tried to summon whatever he needed to tell a story he did not share often, if at all.

"He had a long running feud with this particular group and he never backed down. The animosity built for quite some time. He was stabbed in the back and choked with a chain. The coroner said the knife must have been twelve inches long. Punctured his heart on the other side. The choke was overkill." He stared straight ahead—his face hard—his jaw line as tight as a winch raising a heavy load.

"Where were you?"

Tersely he responded, "In the bathroom. I had the shits that night of all nights."

"Not your fault."

"Sure does feel like it."

"So, you protect Ellie from guys like me because of her dad."

"She doesn't need protection from you. If I thought that your ass would be in jail regardless of what I had to do to get you there. Still…"

"She is married," I finished.

"There is that."

"She is leaving him when he comes home Sunday."

He looked at me in surprise but not shock.

"It's not about me."

"He once was a good guy but he is scum now. Found out a while back that he was keeping company with an older lady across the bridge. She goes out of town with him for work and race trips." He breathed in and exhaled heavily., "I feel like I should tell Ellie but not sure how to go about that one."

"She is pretty wise. Betting that she knows."

"Might be why she is fooling around with you."

"Not for my good looks and all-around charm?"

"Who knows?" he said and offered a slight chuckle.

"Does she know about you?"

He shook his head. "It was a long time ago, and she was a little girl. She just knows me as a cop who works on the Island and checks on her. She doesn't know that I was her dad's partner. And I don't ever want her to know," he said wearily.

"She would never blame you for what happened."

He sighed loudly. "I know. Still…"

"Your secret is safe with me."

His eyes lightened. "Let's get some breakfast."

"You don't need to be seen with me. Not with our history this week."

"Screw that, Bubba, you ain't the only one that walks to the sound of your own voice."

"Own voice," I softly repeated.

He looked at me strangely. "I say something funny?"

"No. Nothing funny at all. Just another time and another place."

"And another woman."

I breathed in and exhaled slowly. "Not just another woman. The woman that would have made life right."

"How long has it been?"

"Not long enough," I responded.

He knew that was the end of the subject. "Breakfast?"

"Only if you tell me your first name. A guy has to have some standards before he accepts a breakfast date."

"Bruce," he replied and extended his hand.

I shook it.

"There is one more thing, Bruce, before I go to breakfast with you."

"What's that?"

"Don't try to slide another Bubba by me."

He chuckled loudly.

We walked toward a small diner on the other side of the parking lot. It was one of those restaurants that every Island town seemed to have. It opened early for breakfast, served lunch, and closed each day by two p.m.

"Are you off today, Bruce?"

"That is affirmative," he answered. "I got an idea. Why don't you stay in tonight and take the night off as well?"

"That is a wise idea. I wonder why I did not think of it."

"Because you ain't as clever as I am."

"One smart ass around here is enough, don't you think?" I asked dryly.

"Maybe so," he replied with a big smile.

"I'm kind of tired anyway."

We were at the door now. Just before he opened it to go inside, he eyed me and winked. "Yeah, only so much drinking, fighting, and screwing that a man your age can handle."

The door closed with me still standing outside. Bruce grinned at me through the glass, reveling in the fact that he got the best of me in the verbal discourse. I shook my head in dismay. Maybe it was a night to stay inside. Obviously, I was not at my best.

Ellie knocked on my door just before midnight. She had left her car at the restaurant and walked the half mile to my house. We undressed and went straight to bed.

In the stillness of the night as our bodies moved like familiar dance partners, I whispered in the darkness. "My age, my ass."

She never heard me.

That was good. I don't know what explanation I would have fashioned that would explain why I was thinking of Bruce at that moment.

Friday

The temperature was eighty degrees and summer beckoned, even though it was not yet May. It was mid-morning and I was sitting on the beach. I stayed in last night much to the relief of Officer Johns, or Bruce, now that we are on a first name basis. I did not stay away from Ellie but that could hardly be construed as my fault. Maybe it would be best to back away for her sake. Perhaps I should be so noble that I could say it was out of some guilt complex that I am suffering but I don't feel that way. It is possible that I should. Okay, skip the possible part. I am supposed to feel remorseful. I'm sleeping with another man's wife. Even someone as far from God as me recognizes the error in that.

She was gone when I woke early this morning. Not even a note left behind. I felt only slightly tawdry.

I brought no book today, which is rare. I stared at the ocean and I reflected on all the times I have gazed at the Atlantic, attempting to piece together the shattered fragments of my life. The sea has proven to be my sanctuary more so than cathedrals.

As I watched the waves roll in and depart again; I reflected that I am like a good but not great boxer with an enormous heart. I have gotten off the canvas many times to fight for another day. Finding hope when it seemed there was none to be found. I am a survivor if nothing else. The question I kept asking myself of late is whether I care enough to answer the bell for one more round.

My cell phone rang, and I see Mira's name light up. I never believed in love at first sight until I met her a few months ago.

I had these expectations of love and relationship for so long that it was the reason I spent so much of my life without the relationship my heart desired. Women came and went. Some left me and I ended it with some of them. There were times that I loved but it never came in the package that I desired. Not until one day I turned around and she was there, walking a chocolate lab, named Belle that she had rescued. Belle was supposed to be our good luck charm since petting her was the excuse I used to talk with her master. It was a fact during our brief time together that she never allowed me to forget.

She was short, barely five feet tall with slightly thick but firm legs. She had long brown hair and amber-colored eyes. She was cute, not beautiful, but something about her just drew me in.

She never got over the fact that I was so smitten with a woman wearing black gym shorts, a gray top, and a Nike baseball cap, that was so worn it was hard to identify the original color. But I was in ways not seen in my time here on this earth.

We connected in a way that was so natural and comfortable that it bordered on surreal at times. I have found myself in situations where I lived more of the woman's life or she lived more of mine. Ultimately that failed to work. In this case, Mira and I seemed to stand together, looking out through similar eyes, with parallel dreams. It is funny the give and take of relationships. The battles for who gives in and who does not. Jada and I use to spar over the simplest of things like whose house were we going to spend the night at. There was never any of that with Mira. I gave in more but I did not mind because I knew that her daughter, Morgan came first, and that was as it should be.

Morgan was eight years old, full of exuberance, and possessed a smile encased in sadness until I entered the room when she would light up as if Santa Claus had appeared in July bearing a sack of unexpected gifts. I can't place into words how special that child made me feel.

Mira's husband died suddenly three years almost to the day we began dating. He awakened one morning to a brain aneurysm that removed him from their world quickly and decisively with no time for good-byes. I wish it would never have happened but we can hope for these things forever and ultimately it is up to those of us left behind that have to find a way to go on living. Even during the difficult times when we might prefer not to. I have been at that point since the day she walked out of my life. She made promises that in her heart that I knew she meant but she could not let go of the guilty feeling that loving me emitted.

Mira backed away after our first week together,

when we were scarcely apart. She relented but ultimately her guilt was more formidable than whatever feelings she carried for me. We were together for one month and I blocked out the thoughts that each moment with her was borrowed time. I wanted to be the one to walk away before she rendered the death sentence to our relationship that I knew was coming, but I also did not want to be the one who made a decision that hurt the little girl I loved so dearly.

She quizzed me once if I felt deserving of what we had. Maybe she should have directed the question at herself. Maybe she did and I missed it. I have asked God a million times why this happened. He has yet to answer.

Mira is building a house at the northernmost end of the county. She is so smart about these things that she serves as her own contractor. Once, I thought I would be going with them. It was the only package in this life that I would have chosen to leave Carolina Beach for.

She phones about once a month to see how I am doing and to update me on Morgan and how the house is coming along. The conversations are short and business-like and I wonder why she does it at all. They were about to move in the last time she called. I don't desire to hear how quiet and peaceful it is looking out over the extensive marshland that serves as their backyard. Each time the call ended I felt hollow and left out. The love I feel for her right now can only be surpassed by how much I detest her.

The phone call I did not take elevates the rage in me that is unmatched this week. Where are three guys to fight when you need them? Hell, I would knock Santa Claus out at this moment on Christmas morning. I rose and packed my stuff. No chance for the solitude the beach often granted. I walked briskly to my truck.

Minutes later I was at home and I can't recall a conscious moment during the short drive home. I put on workout clothes and rolled my bike out of the garage. I put my earbuds in and strapped my I pod on my arm. Mira had a fit that I refused to wear a helmet. I no longer care what she thinks about anything. She could have found the courage to allow us to work together to find our way. Everyone was for us but her. It is a damn shame. I know that I am being unreasonable right now. I don't know what it is like to watch a spouse, the father of your child, die in front of you. She often told me that no one knew what it was like to walk in her shoes and I know she was right. Still, I never asked for the excruciating pain of watching something leave that you feel deep inside that you might never encounter again.

I take off on my bike, pushing hard from the beginning, before stopping quickly. The first song is designed to ease me into the ride. It was a song by my nephew, Paul. He wrote it and recorded it with a band that he played in when he was going to school in Colorado. I loved the song and had visions of him singing it on the beach when Mira and I got married. Morgan standing with us, full of smiles and Micah beside me as my best man. But the fairy tale died and maybe I did along with it. Right now, the song is too damn slow. I skip songs until I find a Pearl Jam mix that I have not listened to in years. That is more like it. I take off once again in a fury.

I rode through the state park and then I pedaled south through mismatched neighborhoods. The early heat of the season along with the intensity of my ride had me pouring sweat. I forgot to pack water in my haste to ride. I always keep spare money in a pouch strapped to my bike. I biked toward a small grocery store and slowed at the side of the building. That is when I saw him. He was skinny, about 6' tall, with long stringy oily black hair. His face is worn and the creases on his face reminded me of crevices on the side of a mountain. He has a friend with him that has long blond hair and looks slightly better than his pal. "Of all days," I muttered.

I jumped off my bike and let it continue rolling without me. It crashed into the pole at the corner of the overhang of the store. The one with dark hair looked up just as I hit him with a right hand so violently it reminded me of a jackhammer breaking concrete. His back slammed into the wall. I refused to let him fall. I held him up and hit him repeatedly. He probably was unconscious after the first blow but I didn't care.

The other guy yelled repeatedly for me to stop and

pulled on my right shoulder, which briefly interrupted my intention to cave this guy's face in. I turned to him. He saw something in my eyes that induced him to flee toward the front door of the store.

I don't know how long I kept hitting him. I felt the nightstick slam into my right shoulder. I dropped the man as a result and turned to see my favorite rookie cop. He was alone. He swung the nightstick viciously at my head. I caught it with my left hand and held it. I looked at him as he struggled to regain control of his weapon. There was astonishment in his eyes and then fear consumed his face.

"I will let go of this and you can handcuff me. I'll go quietly. On that, you have my word. But if you raise this at me again, I will take it away from you and beat you like the spoiled little kid you are and will always be. Are we clear?"

He debated a few moments before he simply nodded his head in agreement. I have such wonderful powers of persuasion these days. Maybe after I get out of jail, I will do my own motivational podcast. Somewhere in the distance, Tony Robbins must be quivering at the thought of the competition.

I held my hands out in front of me.

"Behind you," he said.

"Front or nothing. Your choice."

He stood there dumbfounded—not much of a leap for him as he deliberated on the proper choice.

I thought that I would help him. "Junior, right now I got nothing. You hear me. Nothing to lose," I said very deliberately. "You don't ever want to mess with a man who has nothing else left to lose. I know you are not real bright, but I hope that this is sinking into your fat fricking head. You can handcuff me in front. I will allow that, but not behind me, and if you try to force me you better be ready to shoot a man that has no weapon. Think it through, Junior. I bet whoever is responsible for landing you this job won't be able to save you from something like that." I held my hands out in front again.

He searched my eyes, maybe he was hoping for a sign of weakness or the slightest hint that I might be bluffing. He wasn't going to discover something that did not exist.

"I know you can't keep up with my sterling communication skills but even a moron like you should be able to make the correct choice." I shook my head slightly in frustration. He probably doesn't even know what the word sterling meant in this context. Should I explain that it can mean excellent, exceptional, worthy or outstanding?

Finally, he chose to cuff my hands in front and led me to the patrol car. He opened the back door. There was no front seat ride to be had this time. The ambulance arrived as I was getting into the car.

Two patrol cars pulled in before Junior could start the engine. He got out and met them. I could see them talking but I could not hear anything being said. Not that I cared. I watched the EMT's from the ambulance work on the injured man.

Junior got back inside and started the engine. He drove off and as he did, I looked back at the man the EMT's were trying to help and muttered, "Not my son, asshole."

Later the friend of the man that I tried to cave his head in with my fists told the cops that from the first punch I was saying repeatedly, "Not my son." I have no recollection of that. What I do have is a clear picture of the day I discovered this lowlife scared a young boy because he lacked the courage to deal with me.

It was a Sunday afternoon and I was using less traveled neighborhoods to teach Micah to drive. He was struggling to learn and I was losing patience. We took a break and I took over driving. We stopped in front of this same store to get something to drink. There was a car coming from the opposite direction. There was one empty parking spot out front. I took it. I could have been nice but we were both about the same distance from it.

I went inside, while Micah remained in the car. I walked back out and went to his side and suggested that he drive. He got out and walked around the car and got in the driver's seat. I noticed he was apprehensive, but I wrote it off to his usual nerves when it came to driving. I wish that he was not so nervous, but I was glad that he was not fearless like many kids his age.

He backed out very quickly and cut the wheel too sharply and almost hit the car next to him. "Whoa," I shouted, and he hit the brake just in time to avoid the collision.

A dark-haired drunk man shouted at me not to yell at my son. His blond-haired friend pulled him along and said, "Don't mind him. He's drunk."

I watched them walk on and did not know what to make of it. Micah asked, "Dad, what do I do?"

He was forever getting mixed up about which way to turn the wheel when he backed out. I gave him instructions and he was able to back out without additional excitement. He drove quietly for a while and then I took over and drove him to Tiffany's house.

Later that night I could not get my mind off of the incident and I called to try and reassure him. "Micah, I don't want you to worry about this afternoon. We will get through this. We will just practice more."

"Dad," he said and then paused. "There is something that I did not tell you that happened at the store."

"What?"

"You went inside and that man that yelled at you came to my window and cussed me out for cutting him off for the parking spot. I told him obviously that I was not the one driving. His friend pulled him away and apologized."

"He walked right by me in the store and said

nothing."

"He scared me. I won't ever sit in the car alone in that place again."

It took me a few moments to process all of this. "I guess it is a good thing I did not know any of this. I'd be in jail now for fighting those two guys in the street."

There was resignation in his voice when he stated. "I know. That is why I said nothing."

I had thought earlier that my son was being short on maturity and in actuality he was showing wisdom well beyond his years. I felt ashamed for not knowing better.

"It is okay and the only suggestion I have is that you could have just said I don't feel like driving right now. You could have told me the whole truth later. I just don't want you to ever drive when you are that upset."

"That is right, Dad. I could have done that. I will next time."

I went to the store for the next four Sunday afternoons at the same time. I don't know what I would have done if I would have seen this guy again. Maybe not what I just did, but something, that is for sure. No one messes with my son while there is breath left in me.

I am sitting on the tiny bed in a jail cell for the first time since I was eighteen. Jails don't seem to have changed much. Maybe I will suggest an interior decorator. I dated a really successful one a few years back.

I leaned back against the wall. The rage has departed and my mind is still. There is no conflict, sadness, happiness, guilt, or any emotion that I can think of. Thoughts are not racing through my mind at the speed of bullets fired from a machine gun.

Maybe I should be concerned with whether or not I will get out of jail, but I find myself comfortable in my present accommodations. I sensed someone and looked up to see Junior staring through the bars. "You are lucky those other guys showed up. You would have gotten your ass kicked."

I ignored him because it was easy to do. He wasn't worth the energy. Besides, I was doing time. The only thing missing was some Johnny Cash music. I grew up loving rock and roll, but in my later years, country music lyrics seemed to speak more to my soul. Johnny was flawed and fought his inner demons but was looked upon as a good man. He was even friends with Billy Graham. I would like to think some people might regard me in a similar way. I'm just not a legend, and that is fine by me.

Junior talked for five minutes without drawing wind. I looked away and never looked back in his direction. He was of no concern.

"I think that I will volunteer to take you to the county jail. The back way being the route of choice. There are woods along the way for someone to escape. We will see how tough you are then?"

What we have here is a failure to communicate. I laughed softly at the image of the warden speaking these words to Paul Newman in *Cool Hand Luke*.

"What the hell are you laughing at?"

"So Junior, what you are saying is that you might have a chance against me, assuming of course that I am in handcuffs, while you have all your toys."

"I will get you asshole!" he shouted. His face a most unhealthy glow of dark pink.

"No, you won't, Junior. I don't have handcuffs on and you don't stand a chance. You know this so go away and try to be tough to someone that does not recognize that you are a coward at heart."

He jabbered some more, and he was dismissed from my world. Finally, he stopped abruptly in mid-rant.

It delighted me to see the angry look that Officer Johns gave Junior. On the other hand, after Junior was dismissed, the look of disappointment I procured disturbed me. He opened the cell door and sat on the bunk beside me. Neither of us spoke for several minutes.

"I guess I will have to start smoking. I haven't had one in twenty plus years though. Did you bring me any smokes?"

He had something to say but as unbelievable as it seemed he appeared unmoved by my humor.

"You could have killed him," he said evenly. "Even though Junior isn't worth powdered shit he saved that man's life. He just happened to be riding by. By the time we got the call and responded that guy would probably be dead."

"As it is?"

"Assault. He is going to be okay by the way. Not that you would care."

"And should I?"

He rubbed his hand through his hair. There was great weariness in his voice when he asked, "What set you off like that?"

"A few years back, he terrified my son. I'd beat you to a pulp if you frightened my son."

Our eyes locked for several moments. Neither of us willing to back down. Finally, he sighed deeply. "I have a son as well."

"Micah," I said softly.

"What?"

"My son. His name is Micah."

"Micah," he said, with a nod of his head.

"Trouble is that no one is going to be able to prove that this guy threatened Micah. And…"

"Even if that were not so—I would still be here."

"Yeah," he said, with a pained expression on his face. "Who can I call for you?"

I just shook my head and offered nothing.

"Did Junior do anything that I need to be aware of? Did he get out of line at the store?"

I shook my head. "Junior is just an idiot. I don't think he can help it. He is that kid that always got picked on. That is why he is a cop. He is trying to get back all the beatings and humiliation he received as a kid. You better watch him. Don't let him get you hurt. If he does it to himself—the world is a better place, but..."

"I didn't know you cared."

"Don't tell anyone," I offered sarcastically before adding, "You are a good man Bruce, and I am truly sorry for the difficulty I've caused you this week." I breathed deeply and spoke softly, "In another time we could have been friends and that word friend is one I value highly."

"It's not too late."

"Feels like everything is too late right now."

Tiredly he shook his head and walked away.

Minutes later he returned. "The magistrate has set your bail at $5,000."

"Wow. That is the same bail I received when I got busted for four and a half pounds of pot when I was eighteen. Deja Vu, all over again." I know I am being redundant but it is okay when you do it intentionally. "You would think with inflation and all."

"I think it also helped that the guy you nearly killed has been here about two dozen times. The magistrate said, off the record of course, that you probably did Carolina Beach a huge favor and it was a damn shame that you were not allowed to finish the job. Another bit of advice. That guy will be coming at you for money. Settle with him before the attorneys get hold of him. Do not underestimate that he is a drunk that lives day to day on how to get enough money for booze and tobacco.

Take advantage of his desperation."

I said nothing. "Officer Johns," I heard a voice call from around the corner.

He rose to go see what was wanted of him. He was outside the door when he turned back. "Did you really catch Junior's nightstick in mid-air?"

I studied him. Curious as to how he would know that. Knowing that Junior would never divulge that information.

"Witness is out there," he said as he gestured with a turn of his head. "He was across the street. Junior is pretty good with that nightstick. How did you manage to catch it and stop it from moving toward you?"

I guess at another time I would be impressed with my act as well but presently all I could offer was, "Slow motion. Everything appeared in slow motion." I shrugged my shoulders as if it were not my gift, my fault, whatever the case actually may be.

Bruce walked away. He returned thirty minutes later with my friend, Kelly. She has long blonde hair and stays in marvelous shape. She is the whole package. Strong, tough, independent, but soft and tender to compliment it. The kind of friend who would kick your behind when you needed it or hold you when you were hurting.

She is married to my best friend, Jackson. I'm not real proud of her seeing me in my current state of affairs. I looked away as if somehow, she could not see me and if I looked again maybe she would be gone. Kind of a more mature game of rain, rain, go away that we played as kids when the weather ruined our chances to play ball.

I turned back and she was still there. "Go away."

"The hell with you," she answered deliberately. Now I had done it. I pissed her off. Far worse than that there were tears in her eyes. I am in trouble.

Officer Johns opened the cell door and Kelly walked in and sat beside me.

"You can't do that! She can't be in there!"

Once again, my beloved cop, Junior had emerged. Officer Johns closed his eyes wearily. "So help me God son, if you don't get out of here and shut your mouth, I will not be responsible for what I do next."

Bruce opened his eyes and Junior was gone. I wondered briefly why that did not work with Kelly. I reasoned swiftly because she unlike Junior is unafraid.

He turned back to us. "I can't leave her here alone with you but whatever you guys say I won't ever repeat."

"I know that."

The mood in the tiny area of my restriction was somber. It was as if the weight of the world had pressed down on the little cell. Bruce found a metal folding chair, positioned it outside the cell and sat.

"Ma'am…"

"Kelly," she interrupted.

"Kelly," he repeated. "You don't have a weapon of any sorts, do you?"

"I might," she said without expression. "You want to

search me?"

"No ma'am."

"Where have you been, Billy?" she asked as she placed her hand on my shoulder. I winced and drew back. "What did I do?"

Bruce stood and walked to me. "Take your shirt off," he asked in an even voice.

I appealed to him with my expression not to ask again.

"Please," he said, his voice low, barely audible.

I struggled to remove my shirt. Kelly helped me with the last part.

"Remember when we all lived together?" I asked her.

She nodded and as she looked at my new injury courtesy of Junior, along with the other remnants of my week. She cried softly.

"Do you remember the time Jackson was out of town and I got the flu? I was throwing up all night."

"And I slept through it."

"But when you woke you took care of me. You went to the drug store and got me some medicine and Gatorade. And Micah took his television from his room and moved it to mine so I could have something to do."

"You are a pretty woman but you looked terrible that morning."

There was silence and Bruce took the opportunity to inspect my newest mishap. "That's from the nightstick?"

He phrased it as a question but we both knew it was not.

"It's okay. You were right. I would have beaten that guy to death if he wouldn't have stopped me."

"Yeah," he said as he sighed. "But he doesn't even try another way."

"How does he keep his job?"

"Small town politics," he answered jadedly.

He nodded his head and wearily said, "I think that I will have a talk with Junior."

"Let it go."

"Would you?"

"Sure," I lied. But it was not a real lie because he knew the truth. Maybe it was like Forrest Gump said about endorsing the ping pong paddle that he did not use. Mama said it was just a little white lie. My conscious was clear. I could move on. It doesn't take much these days.

He left and returned quickly. He placed a bag of ice on my newest injury. Kelly placed her hand on it to hold it there for me. She smiled at Bruce. "Thank you, Officer Johns."

"Bruce," he replied.

"Thank you for taking care of my good friend."

"I am going to check on the paperwork." He walked away. He didn't even close the door completely. I felt a little like Otis on the *Andy Griffith* show.

"What paperwork?"

"To get you out of here."

"I think this might be where I belong."

"You want to repeat that?" she said sternly.

She had a point. I had not come up against anyone as tough as her this week.

"Man has got to know his limitations," I said.

"Who said that?" she asked with a puzzled expression.

"I just did."

"No," she replied, obviously annoyed. "What movie?"

"Kelly, I know that you often are one of the guys, and I love you for it, but for the love of God don't start quoting movies like we do. Someone has to live in reality. We need that. It keeps us grounded."

"I hung out with all Jackson's friends so much what do you expect?" She paused before continuing. "We haven't seen much of you this year. That thing with Mira really cut deep."

"I don't want to talk about her."

"Honey, she had her husband die in front of her. She had to raise her child alone. Cut her some slack."

"How did you know I was here?"

"Someone got word and called Jackson and he called me and don't think I don't know you are directing the conversation away from Mira."

"Is he upset with me?"

"Jackson? Are you nuts? He said to me and I quote. 'You go down there and get him out of jail right this minute. Like I wouldn't have done it anyway," she added dryly.

Moments passed before she said gently, "I love you. You have always been there for Jackson and me."

"Goes both ways."

Only Junior, the town idiot, could diminish such a moment.

"Get away from him and get out of this cell."

Kelly looked at him without expression. I just shook my head slightly in dismissal, and looked back to Kelly.

The lack of any type of response or acknowledgment must have pushed him over the edge, though I suspected that it was a short trip.

"I'll get you!" he screamed. "I don't care what I have to do. I will get you so help me God." He was in a full-blown temper tantrum like a disobedient two-year-old. This was out of control even for someone of Junior's emotional welfare. He was threatening me in front of a witness. Actually, more than one.

I smiled broadly at him.

"What the hell are you smiling at?"

"The officer standing behind you."

He replied, "Yeah, right," and in the next moment, he was face first into the bars of the unoccupied cell next to me. His arm was twisted behind his back and I was concerned that Bruce might wedge his face in between the bars. Okay, maybe I was not that troubled at all. Besides, I am fairly certain that Junior's face was too plump to fit.

"I am sick and tired of you masquerading as a police officer. You run around here with your bad attitude and hitting people with that damn nightstick. Did you even identify yourself as an officer before you hit him?"

I recognized a good rhetorical question when I hear one. I hope that Junior does as well if he values his face. I was behind Bruce now. I placed my hand on his shoulder.

"Let him go, Bruce. He is not worth it."

At least a minute passed and no one moved. Finally, Bruce released him.

Junior moved away quickly—fear impressed profoundly on his face. There was also a stain on the front of his pants. I was just about to suggest something when Kelly as she is apt to do beat me to the punch.

"Go change your pants," she stated evenly as if she were talking to the third graders that she taught. Junior looked at his pants and then hurried from the area like a frightened child.

"Paperwork is done," Bruce said as he turned to me. "Let's get you out of here."

I gave Bruce the ice bag and slipped my shirt back on. Kelly and I walked outside into the effulgent sunshine. We got into her Chevy Tahoe.

I was tired and sore. I had to hand it to Junior. If nothing else he could swing a nightstick. My shoulder where he struck me was throbbing.

I asked Kelly for her cell phone. I dialed my doctor's

number and was told that he was gone for the day. I was looking forward to getting a prescription of Percocet and it appeared as if I was going to have to settle for Ibuprofen. That is kind of like thinking you have a date with Jennifer Lopez and Rosie O'Donnell showed up.

We rode in silence to my house. She cut the engine off and said softly, "Come home with me. I'll take care of you. Jackson will be back tomorrow. It will be like olden times." It was a lame attempt at an imitation of Forrest Gump.

"We would be like peas and carrots," I said, continuing the Gump dialogue.

"That we would be."

I said nothing.

"But you won't come, will you?"

"Can't believe I am saying no to a woman with your eloquent charm, but I must remain here on the Island. It might be bad luck to venture off of it."

"Probably more likely that it is bad luck for you to remain on the Island the way your body looks."

Shrewdly I switched from *Forrest Gump* to *Tombstone*. "I am in my prime," I replied in my best Val Kilmer/Doc Holiday imitation.

"Yeah, you look it, lunger." It was a line from Johnny Ringo delivered to Doc Holiday. I can't recall if she has the line in perfect sequence or not but I will not quibble with her on this fact, seeing as she does not appear to be thrilled with me at the present time.

"Thank you." I leaned over and kissed her on the cheek.

I glanced to my front door. My bike had beaten me home. It was propped up against the house beside the door along with my iPod and earbuds.

"I love you, Kelly."

"I know. I love you."

"Don't be disappointed in me. It's no secret that there are not many people left in this world that I care what they think of me."

"I know that as well."

"You are still mad at me anyway?"

She shook her head. "I'm glad to be one of those people. There is nothing in this world you would not do for Jackson and me. Except maybe stay in this truck and let me keep you safe."

"I'm going inside. What is not safe about that?"

"It's when you venture out again that worries me." She had her hands on the steering wheel and she was shaking her head as if she were having a private conversation. I bring that out in people. I think it is maybe yet another of my many talents.

"I wish things would have worked out with Mira. I never saw you that way about anyone. You would have moved continents for her and her child."

I forced a disingenuous laugh at a painful memory. She was not fooled by my laughter.

"What?"

"That is what she told me once. That she would move continents for me. I think that was about three days before she decided she was not ready and might never be."

"You still got time. A fine strapping man like you."

"I am not sure I care to try again."

"Have you been seeing anyone at all?"

"Married lady."

"You are not kidding, are you?" She shook her head in dismay.

"This too shall pass."

"Maybe not," she said as she cranked the engine and put the vehicle in reverse. I think that was my cue to get out.

I watched her drive away. A dream that haunted me several times as a child revisited at that moment.

There were parts of my family standing outside a small cinder block building that served as the Community Center in Sea Gate, a small community, in Wilmington, where I was raised. The building rested on property that contained a baseball field. It sat off to the side of left field.

The dream centered on an event that took place in the building but that part was never clear, nor important. There were many family members present and they begin taking off in different cars. My two oldest sisters were both driving by that time and I frequently rode with them instead of my parents.

It was assumed by each of them that I was riding with someone other than them. I kept thinking that there was a car left for me but then everyone departed and I stood alone. I looked out at the field and a chilled wind that felt like the first cold north wind of winter appeared without warning and blew through the field and my soul. The barren baseball field turned to an already harvested field of dried cornstalks as far as the eye could see and I felt more abandoned, more fearful than any child should ever feel. I woke each time after I stared at those cornstalks indefinitely. No one was coming for me and I knew it without question. I never shared the dream with anyone.

As I stood in the drive, I could see those tall, dried, barren cornstalks off in the distance. I felt the icy wind from the nightmare, even though it was eighty degrees.

I walked inside and opened a cabinet and pulled out a bottle of Absolute Vodka. I poured a strong drink, mixed with Fresca, and a slice of lime. I begin to drink in hopes that I could erase the sentiment that haunted me.

After several stiff drinks I was not only still sober— far worse than that. I felt as alone as the kid in the nightmare.

SATURDAY
Streaks of light from the false dawn filtered through the windows. I sat on the loveseat with my feet propped

on the ship's hutch, which served as a living room table. The wood is dense and streaked with different shades of brown. An ordained minister who once worked on my staff was helping with a project at my parents' house. He saw the wood and asked why it was stored away unused. To tell the truth, at the time, I had forgotten it was there. I explained the dilemma that I never found legs sturdy enough to adequately support the heavy weight of it. He asked if we could take it back to the shop and give him time to think of something proper. I shrugged my shoulders noncommittally. He lifted it without further debate and placed it in the back of the truck.

He was a hardworking man who struggled to make ends meet for his family and yet he always seemed to have a grin plastered on his face. He was a bit heavy, with a head full of hair that had turned solid gray long before its time. He loved to work with wood. He was gifted in that regard and more. The younger guys on the crew quickly grew to respect him despite their opposite lifestyles. He never preached. He never corrected. He just lived and smiled and walked out his walk of faith with great humility. I don't know if it was me or someone else but we nicknamed him Rev and in time it was difficult to recall his real name. I think it was Richard, though I am not certain of that on a morning when I am not sure of anything. He built legs in a boxed fashion that I would never have thought to do. I looked at the legs and smiled with the thoughts of such a good man crossing my path that I will in all likelihood never see again.

The smoke alarm in the hallway chirped with the warning that the battery was low. Why don't they ever start chirping in the daytime? It is always in the middle of the night, with the chirps spaced neatly apart to keep you from being able to sleep. The beeping began producing the clamor about three a.m. and in my present state I have been able to tune it out pretty well.

I rose and positioned a bar stool under the smoke alarm. I know you won't believe this but I gracefully stepped on top of the stool. I snatched the battery out and snapped the cover back on and returned to my previous position.

I debated as to why I always desired more, unwilling to compromise my life with the mediocrity that governed others. Women had come through my life at a steady rate but there was always something missing, except for one. I glanced next to me at the empty seat. A loveseat. Little in this life seems designed for one.

I should be passed out but I am not. I should be hung over but physically I feel okay. My head does not even hurt. What a week it has been. I belted that guy in the restaurant Sunday, and I capped it by nearly beating a man to death yesterday. Oh, and throw in that I had an affair with a married woman. I don't even think Rev could be silent if he knew about it. He left long ago to move to Alabama for hopefully better opportunities as well as being closer to family.

A loud cracking noise struck the window to my right. Debating briefly and deciding that I was not yet suffering alcoholic delusions; I rose and walked outside to the front porch. There was a small grayish bird with a speck of yellow on his throat lying on the concrete, staring wide eyed at a life known until seconds ago. I found it ironic to see both beauty and death intertwined. Somehow it seemed an applicable way to begin my day.

I walked to the garage and retrieved a shovel. I buried the bird in a plant bed just off the porch near a mix of ornamental grasses.

As I looked at the freshly dug grave, thoughts of Mira and that desolate field of corn from the tormented dream of my youth fused. Why that seems to fit with the demise of this bird proves a mystery.

§

It was early evening and the sun hung low in the faded blue sky that is splashed with a brilliant array of colors, ranging from yellow to pink. I was sitting outside at one of our local restaurants. There was a band consisting of guys in their fifties preparing to entertain us. They don't look like rockers, and I would bet my home they are a beach music band. I have to confess that even though it is argued that beach music originated right in this very area. I have never cared for it.

I thought I might at some point nap today but I never did feel the need. The young waitress stopped at my table. Her hair is long, dark and the perfect hair you see in a shampoo commercial. She has vast dark eyes, flawless tanned skin, and a smile reserved for garnering tips. They can flirt with me all they want but even my oversized ego does not allow me to believe that I am attractive to a girl in her early twenties.

I touched my Modelo bottle easily and she nodded. "I will be right back."

She wore a short black skirt with a cherry-colored top that ended midway between her elbow and wrist. She is also quite firm in the butt and legs department.

"Like looking at my girl, old man?" I turned to the sound of the voice. He has long blond hair and is far too skinny to be talking to me this way. His courage fueled by alcohol and his cohorts. I turned away—deciding to allow them to live.

Life is what it is. I can wish that Mira would not have done what she did but it is to no avail. I can pray that God would make a way for me to pay for Micah to go to that school. The end results will prove the same.

She was back with my beer. I thanked her.

"Did you hear me, old man?" Laughter came from all three as they punched each other like juvenile delinquents.

She looked at their table and back at me and was none too pleased. "I'm sorry," she offered.

"No worries. As long as they stay over there and behave like fools it is fine but if they venture this way your boyfriend needs to know something."

Her breathing paused for a moment. "What should he know?" she asked hesitantly.

"I tell you what—let's go over there and I will tell him."

"I can't afford to lose my job. Please don't."

"I don't want that either."

I rose and walked to the table and pulled out a chair and sat. She followed me and stood to the side. I think I had their attention. My eyes ignored the other two guys and I honed in on the one I wished to converse with. "Your girlfriend doesn't need you causing trouble over nothing more than your desire to impress your pals by making fun of someone. It is at my expense and I think you should know something."

He was nervous. I could tell by his darting eyes and the constant licking of his lips. He tried to be brave but even with the company of his friends, he was fearful. He wanted to go back in time and make a different decision than the one that had led him down this particular path. A decision that would not lead to having a stranger with no fear in his eyes sitting across from him. He will learn in time that we don't get a do over in life. I wish we did, though I wouldn't know just where to begin in my case.

"What should I know?" he asked in a futile attempt to sound brave. His words offered in a rush. He swallowed nervously. This guy wanted people to think he was cool. You could just see it down to his short sleeve buttoned floral tropical shirt.

"Don't allow your mouth to overload your ass." I delivered the words evenly, without expression.

He started to speak but refrained.

His girlfriend stood nervously by. "What's your name?" I asked as I looked up to her.

"Erin," she answered.

"Erin, bring these gentlemen another round and put it on my tab."

She looked at me hesitantly.

"They will be here when you return, and unharmed, including your boyfriend. On that, you have my word."

She examined me closely. I nodded once and smiled slightly. Hesitantly, she walked away.

We sat quietly, which was fine by me. In the distance, I heard bagpipes and smiled.

Her boyfriend asked, "What is that?"

"Bagpipes," I replied softly.

"Oh, the guys who wear those dresses."

I shook my head faintly. "They are called kilts. Take a walk with me," I said as I rose from the table.

He did not budge.

"C'mon," I said lightly. "I gave my word to Erin, and I don't break promises."

He stood and looked at his friends.

"You guys tell Erin we will be right back, okay?"

They nodded but did not speak.

We walked toward the sound of the bagpipes.

Minutes later we were at the end of a walkway that crossed over the dunes. I sat down on the steps and he joined me.

We watched in silence as the man in the plaid kilt walked down the beach playing music so beautiful, so soothing, that I was certain that I was witnessing something so picturesque, so delicate, that it seemed misplaced among the cruelty that is my present life.

"What's your name?"

"Jason," he answered.

I stretched out my hand and shook his. "Billy."

"That is pretty cool, isn't it?"

"That is exactly what it is."

We sat and listened without additional words. Periodically, I glanced over and saw a look of appreciation on his face.

The beach was still and there was no one in sight except for the bagpipe player who seemed to have been sent by God to play just for us. The music proved soothing. I reflected again on my week and decided in that moment that I was going to New York just as my officer friend had so succinctly suggested. I would book a flight and depart tomorrow.

The sun was lower as the man drifted away from us. His music trailed faintly behind him.

"Let's head back before your girlfriend gets too nervous."

"Yeah, she probably thinks that I am dead by now."

As we rose and began walking back toward the restaurant, I thought it best not to tell him that I did indeed almost kill a man yesterday.

We were sitting at the table when Erin returned with our drinks. She had already served the other two young men while she waited. The relief on her face was quite evident when she saw Jason unscathed.

"I told you I would not hurt him." I took my beer and rose to return to my table.

"Thanks for the drink," Jason offered.

"You are welcome."

"Yeah, thanks," his two buddies mumbled.

My back was turned to them when I heard one of them ask, "You could have taken all three of us couldn't you?"

I turned back to them. "Yes," I answered evenly. "Sometimes you get lucky and learn a lesson and no one gets hurt."

I think all three of the boys understood and Erin smiled, and whispered a voiceless, "Thank you."

It strikes me that I have not eaten a thing all day. "Can I order some food?"

"You certainly may. What can I get you?"

"The grilled grouper wrap and onion rings."

She smiled broadly. "That is my favorite thing on the menu."

The band began to play and of course, they played "Carolina Girls," one of the most nauseating, and the most copied beach music song by cover bands everywhere. I returned to my table.

Minutes later I was eating a tasty meal and enjoying another Modelo. Even better the band was having a technical problem and was forced to cease playing. In a week when I had experienced every conceivable emotion, I believe that I had reached a truce with this life. The anger entirely dissipated and I did not think that it would return. My brief stint as a fighter was hopefully over.

I nursed a few beers and decided to call it a night. The sun had surrendered its light for the day, and I was finally tired. I knew it would be one of those rare, glorious nights that I would be out as soon as my head hit the pillow. Jason had sent a couple of beers over and silently toasted me from across the floor.

I left Erin a fifty-dollar tip and walked over to their table and offered my hand. Jason stood and shook it and said, "Thanks for everything. These are my friends, Ryan and Wes." I shook their hands.

Jason looked at me and said, "I'm sorry I showed my ass earlier. I was out of line."

He was sincere—his apology from the heart. "Jason, there are not many men that have the integrity to apologize and mean it." I turned to his friends. "Have a good night."

I walked toward the back wooden gate as the band continued to play. Their technical issues unfortunately did not last long enough. I was almost out of the door when I heard Erin and then felt her hand on my shoulder.

I turned toward her. She smiled beautifully. "Thank you for the tip. It is too much."

I shook my head. "No, it is not. It is what is right."

"I bet you are big on what is right."

"It still gets confusing at times—even for an old guy like me."

"You are still handsome."

"That is as big a tip as you are going to receive young lady."

She laughed freely. She paused before adding, "Jason is a nice guy. He treats me well and never would disrespect me. The three of them have been friends since grammar school. They tend to get a little too full of themselves when they get together."

"Why share this with me?"

"I saw the way Jason looked at you as you were leaving. The respect was evident." She paused before adding, "I just don't want you to think badly of him. His old man was a drunk that beat his mom regularly."

"You said was."

"Excuse me."

"You said his old man was a drunk."

"He died last year in a head on collision. He crossed the center line and hit a minivan with a mom and two small girls. Everyone involved in the accident died."

"He is a very fortunate young man to have you."

She grinned quickly. "I know that."

It was quiet confidence without a hint of arrogance.

"I have to go. Thank you for everything." She hugged me tightly and then bounced away.

My eyes made contact with Jason and he was smiling warmly. I nodded and turned back to the door.

I entered the parking lot and looked at my truck. I knew it was better not to drive and it was only a mile walk to my house.

I walked for a few minutes and chose to walk the back-route home, which meant going down St. Joseph Street. Maybe there would be a light on at Ellie's. I dismissed that thought quickly and decided it was best to move on from her. It was for her sake more than mine. She was at a crossroads in her life, and she did not need me around to muddy the waters. Ah, in another time and another place, I waxed philosophically. Besides, my heart belonged to another and though it was not going to happen for us that did not remove the feeling that still presided over my heart.

That could be removed only with time, be it ever so measured and painful. But that day would come when it would no longer matter. And rushing the process would only delay that time when all that remained was a scar.

What day had Mira called? I couldn't recall right now. The week seemed now as if it were one long day. I thought of Morgan and at this moment. I missed her even more than I did her mom. She had no choice in the matter. She wanted me but her mother chose another path. Maybe I have been too hard on Mira. I have such a life where lasting love was the crowning jewel that I desired and to have a real chance at that and walk away because of the past I couldn't comprehend. It would be easier if I could remain convinced that she just did not love me the way she professed. Sometimes I was successful but tonight I can see her eyes clearly and they are lost inside of me. My body is bruised and battered and yet it does not hold a candle to the pain, to the yearning for her that permeates in my heart.

A car passed by that contained three men. I noticed the passenger had long dirty blond hair but then my thoughts fell back to the petite woman who brought me to my knees. I gazed at the stars and whispered, "You could have helped, God." I chuckled and reflected for the millionth time on why the big guy put us here. I have heard a thousand explanations and none of them have ever sufficed. People spend so much time explaining God. The answers crammed neatly in a box slightly smaller than the confines of their minds. The reality is our questions far exceeded the answers we possessed.

I passed the old movie theater. I am going to New York tomorrow to see my son. I took my cell phone out of my shorts pocket and sent the signal.

"Dad," he answered.

"I was thinking about coming to see you tomorrow."

"Well, stop thinking, end this call, and book a flight."

"I take it that it would be okay."

"It is more than okay. Call me when you know what time you will be here. We will have dinner tomorrow, and I will show you the sights."

I smiled at his eagerness to see me. "I will call you tomorrow. I love you."

"I love you too. I'm so excited that you are coming. Bye."

"Bye," I replied and clicked off the call.

I neared the entrance of a neighborhood of nice town homes and single homes. The entrance is maturely landscaped, and the road is paved in brick. There were large dense shrubs along the wall. I looked that way and felt a strange feeling but dismissed it and returned to my newfound happier thoughts.

I sensed movement to my left but it was too late. I caught a glimpse of dirty blond hair and the smell of tobacco and poor hygiene. Quickly, I backed away but not far enough. The knife swept across my rib cage on my left side. He ran back toward the movie theater as I bent down, clutching my side, and felt the warm blood.

I saw the taillights of a car through the trees. They had been smart. They parked in back of the theater and now were driving toward the main highway. There was no way I would get a glimpse of the vehicle.

The blood did not seem to be spurting, which I considered to be good. Still, this was no paper cut. I tried to see the damage in the dark but I couldn't. What do I do next? The smart move is to call 911. No, I was not going to do that.

The pain was coming in waves. I thought I might throw up. I began to breathe deeply and I continued walking in the same direction the best I could. Every few steps I paused to garner strength.

I managed to make it to Ellie's and walked around to the back door. Her husband would be home tomorrow, but it was tonight and I needed her.

I knocked and she took her time walking to the door. She looked defiantly at me through the glass in the door.

"Go away," I heard her say, but her voice was muddled. It sounded as if someone was talking into a can. The nausea hit again. The most powerful wave yet. I dropped to my knees and fell lazily to the wooden deck beneath me.

The door opened. "Stop playing and go home." The next thing I heard was "Oh, my God." She ran back inside.

"No," I yelled.

She was back now and I gave her my best smile but the pain cut it short. I lifted my hand toward her. "Help me up please."

She extended her hand and put an arm around my back and helped me to my feet. She led me to the kitchen and pulled a chair out for me to sit. She walked to the bedroom and retrieved her phone and returned. "I am calling 911."

"You do realize that there will be a report and that your neighbors will see an ambulance. What kind of story are you going to spin for why I was in your house? No need to give your husband that kind of information even if you follow through on your decision to leave him. Please let's look at it first."

She placed the phone on the counter and went to the restroom. She returned with an emergency kit. She began to work on the wound, cleaning it diligently but as tenderly as she can manage. "This is going to hurt," she said, and then she soaked the wound in alcohol.

I winced but I am a tough guy so I did not scream. The blood had slowed. "Just a long oyster cut, right?"

She failed to reply.

"You know what you are doing, don't you?"

"Dad died when I was ten. Mom worked two jobs to support us. I had two little brothers that were as adventuresome as you. They had youth to blame. I am not sure what you can offer for an excuse."

"Not youth?"

I received the glare she routinely dished out but she does not mean it. Hell, I am suave enough, even when I am not bleeding.

"Did you search for trouble again?"

"Believe it or not I was having a nice peaceful night.

Earlier, I sat on the beach and listened to a man play bagpipes."

She looked at me sternly like you would a small child. That is probably how she looked at her little brothers when they told her something that seemed far fetched.

There was silence as I watched her apply several butterfly bandages to pull the cut together. She looked up from her work. "It's not too deep," she said as she added two additional butterfly bandages. "Do you know who it was?"

I said nothing.

"I will take that as a yes."

"I didn't know that you had two little brothers."

She wrapped gauze along the wound and then taped it snugly with medical tape. "Lots you don't know about me."

I gently touched her face. "Lots I do know as well."

She nodded.

"Will you do two things for me?"

"What?" she asked sharply.

"I need a drink of that vodka on the counter and four Advil."

She poured three fingers of Broken Shed Vodka into a glass and got the meds I requested out of the container that was beside the bottle. I swallowed the pills and felt the burn of the Vodka in the back of my throat. It's probably been ten years since I drank liquor straight. I drank half of it and placed the glass on the table. She picked it up and finished it.

"The other thing," I said.

"What other thing? You said two things. Vodka and Advil," she said tersely.

I struggled to contain my irritation. "Could you stop being so damn hard for just one minute?"

She said nothing. I took that as a good sign. "Kiss me," I asked softly, and she did. I tasted the Vodka on our breath.

"Thank you. Can you take me home?"

"No, you will stay here tonight, and then you can never see me again. Don't call. Don't come to the restaurant. No contact. I will do anything you ask tonight. I will not call 911 unless you start bleeding again."

"I will if you promise me something and that you never break the promise."

She eyed me curiously. "What?"

"Never think badly of me."

"That matters to you?" Her eyes were opened wider than usual as she observed me. Maybe she thought by doing so it might help her look deeper inside of me. I started to tell her that it wouldn't help.

"It matters a lot."

"I have no reason to think badly of you. You are a good and gentle man. I don't care how many fights you have been in this week. Violence is not your nature. And that woman..."

"Mira," I interrupted.

"Mira was and is a damn fool. She had a chance at unconditional love with a man like you. A man that would always mean it when he said he loves you. Those three words would never become a way of saying goodbye. They would always be sincere. A man that would love her on the good days and the bad." She poured some more vodka into the glass and whispered, "Possibly even more on the bad days.

"I'm going to wash your clothes and get the blood out the best I can. You don't need to be seen like this." Stand up and let me get your shorts off.

I did as she requested.

"Might as well give me the underwear. There is blood on them as well."

"That might lead to something else," I slyly suggested as she helped me remove them.

She moved closer and said, "Whatever you do, don't strain and you will promise me that tomorrow morning you will go to the ER or at least the urgent care down the road." She looked at me with a stern expression daring me to disagree with her last statement.

I very gently nodded in agreement.

"Go lie down in my bed. I will start these clothes and I will join you shortly."

Soon after we enjoyed each other for what we both knew was our last time—I fell asleep quickly and deeply and into a dream where I was standing on the shore, gazing at the ocean. It was the color of teal—the waves as white as freshly falling snow. A pod of porpoises surfed the waves.

I have no idea how long I slept. Minutes, hours? But I woke with her head nestled on my chest. She snored softly as I enjoyed the moments of tranquility, which are fleeting at best in this whirlwind mind of mine. I breathed in deeply—the peacefulness washing over me.

There was music playing off in the distance. The music was moving and I knew that it was coming from one of the party boats heading back to the marina. I swear it was the Eagles and the song was "Peaceful Easy Feeling." How appropriate is that?

EPILOGUE
(11:49 p.m.)

And now we return to the beginning of this little story and what has proven to undoubtedly be the most tumultuous week of my life. As I stared without concern at the weapon aimed at me, I am convinced that God really was winking at me the past few months as I drove behind numerous vehicles with one brake light burned out.

"I am going to blow your bleeping brains out." Now you know he didn't say bleeping. I referred once again to *The Christmas Story* and chicken man did not say bleeping any more than Ralphie said fudge. This brought to mind a debate as to the versatility of curse words. The word he just used I once considered it to be the most versatile word in the English language, though my mom got multiple usages from the word shit. The big difference was that she never considered shit a cuss word but if I would have said, well fudge, in front of her as a child she would have knocked me silly. I looked at the clock on the wall. The bizarre week is near the end and I might be as well. As with most things of late, I don't give a shit. That is definitely one line where shit is the superior word to be used. Score one for mom. Well, score two for her as she asked me a few years back not to use that word that Ralphie said during the flawed tire change scene, either in her presence or not. I have done my best to comply. Mothers sure have a hold on their southern boys.

"You said that," I answered dryly, returning to the scene at hand.

"You have been sleeping with my wife." He moved closer and raised the gun to my face. "Get down on your knees."

"No."

His finger moved slightly against the trigger. "You don't think I will?"

"I don't know. You may or you may not and I can go either way with your decision. What you can be rest assured of is that I will not under any circumstances get down on my knees and beg to a man that has the face of a chicken."

"Billy, please," Ellie pleaded.

His eyes left mine and he looked at his wife.

"I was going to leave you anyway."

"Why?" he asked as if the idea never occurred to him that his wife might not be completely blissful with their current state of matrimony.

"Emmitt. Why would I want to stay?"

And he made fun of my name?

"This is your fault," he said as he returned his hard stare in my direction.

"Part of it," I responded with a slight shrug of my shoulders. "And part of it is yours, and probably part of it hers."

"You got an answer for everything don't you?"

"Almost."

I thought about my plans to see Micah. Too bad I didn't book the flight for today. I could have saved getting stabbed, which would have meant I would not be here looking down the barrel of a pistol. None of that mattered because I am where I am. I made the choices that led to this. I noticed his hand tighten and the scene played out in slow motion.

I saw the bullet leave the barrel of the gun. I know that is not physically possible but just the same—I assure you that I could see the bullet spinning toward me. And at that moment I thought of what mattered most, Micah. He was going to have no more financial worries in his life for quite some time. He could attend that college and enhance his acting skills. My second thought was of Mira and how my heart would grieve no longer. And then I saw the bullet no longer because it had entered into my chest.

I fell to the floor. Emmitt stood over me and his face changed from one of a killer to one more closely resembling a small boy that had received a failing grade on his report card, and whose face was filled with terror at the whipping he was certain to receive when his father came home. The realization of the act he had just committed dawned on him. He dropped the gun and ran quickly out the door. If I would have had the strength, I would have told him that you can't outrun a nightmare.

Ellie grabbed a towel, dialed 911, and put the phone on speaker as she pressed the towel firmly against my chest. I heard a vehicle start from far away. Emmitt had parked down the street and walked here because he knew his woman was not being faithful. Some things you just know. I have been down that road as well. There is not much that I have missed out on in this life. I heard sirens in the distance. They would be here soon. The station was just off the Island, on the other side of Snow's Cut Bridge. I thought of the high-rise bridge and when you reached the crest it is often difficult to decide which direction to look. On one side you can see the Cape Fear River and on the other the Atlantic Ocean. Snow's Cut Inlet runs underneath. If the sun is bedding down on the river, I always choose to look in that direction. I recalled the most beautiful time I ever crossed the bridge. I was leaving the Island one cold January morning. It snowed the night before. A rarity in our area. The steep banks of the Inlet and the trees behind it were covered in pristine snow. The scene brought to mind the wonderful art of Bob Timberlake. I have seen much beauty in my life and I realize now that it would have been better to enjoy it, rather than to clutch it and attempt to make it my own.

The sirens grew louder. I have laid in bed at night many times and heard similar sirens and speculated as to where it might be going. Tonight, I know just where the ambulance is heading, but it will be too late.

"Stay with me, baby," she pleaded. She was holding

the towel firmly with one hand and rubbing my head with the other.

"Not idiot," I said wearily.

Her tears were falling on me and she touched my face with hers. "The ambulance is on the way. Please don't give up."

"I'm tired, Ellie. I just want to go to sleep."

"No!" she shouted sharply.

"Make sure Jackson is the one to call Micah. His number is in my phone."

"Don't leave," she pleaded.

I heard the front door open and the sound of footsteps moving quickly across the floor. Bruce was kneeling over me.

"Hey, Bruce. I got knifed and shot all in the same night. That is pretty good even for my standards."

He turned to Ellie and saw the blood splattered on her clothes. "Are you okay?"

She nodded through a torrent of tears.

"They picked Emmitt up on the other side of the bridge." He turned back to me. "Did he knife you also?"

I was weak and I could feel life leaving me in phases. I managed to shake my head no.

"Who did it?"

I deliberated for several moments. "If I tell you, will you play it my way and not arrest him?"

His face was a mask of confusion.

"It would be for Micah."

His face cleared and he said softly, "Tell me. I promise that I will do the best that I can."

"The friend of the guy I put in the hospital. Maybe his friend will want to keep him from jail and the others in the car."

Bruce's eyes opened wider with a look of intrigue. "He refused to stay in the hospital. Couldn't do without alcohol and cigarettes. No way he would miss out on not being along for the ride. Why don't you want me to arrest him?"

I felt blood in the back of my throat and it occurred to me that I was drowning in my own blood. "Hold my head up Ellie, please."

She positioned herself behind me and lifted my head gently and placed it in her lap. "I want you to hold it over him so that if he seeks one dime from my estate both of them will be arrested, along with the driver." I struggled to continue. I breathed deeply and began again. "I'm sure you will find a way to convince them that you have the goods on them."

"I can't..."

"Micah," I muttered as I gasped for breath. I reached out and took his hand and gripped it with all that I had left in me. At this point, it was probably equivalent to the third-graders that Kelly taught.

He gripped my hand and merely nodded and that was all the assurance that I needed.

"What time is it?"

He glanced at his watch. "About a half minute from midnight."

"Quite a week."

He knelt beside me and said quietly, "The ambulance is almost here."

I smiled and said, "I don't think it will matter much."

I closed my eyes, and the light flickered and then it was gone and I with it.

§

"I can't sleep, Mom."

Mira was sitting in a white wicker couch outside on the upper deck of the newly completed house. She turned to her precious daughter. She stood before her wearing a long sleeve tee shirt that served as pajamas. She beckoned for her and pulled her in close, holding her tightly.

"Why are you crying?" Morgan asked innocently.

Mira shook her head.

"Because as great as our new house is it is not as great without Mr. Billy here. Mom, I miss him. He did not just love you. He loved me," she stated matter-of-factly.

"How do you know that?"

"You could see it in his eyes and by the way he talked to me."

Morgan pulled slightly away from her and looked into her mother's eyes. "You know how adults talk to kids like we are stupid? Mr. Billy talked to me like I was a person. Not just a child."

The old antique clock inside began signaling that it was midnight. A cold breeze came out of nowhere and as Mira clutched her child, she felt a chill inside of her that caused her to shudder uncontrollably.

Strangely, she recalled a time she lived in the Midwest where cornfields were abundant. As she looked out toward the marshlands all she could see were harvested cornstalks that all life had dissipated from. She bowed her head and wept bitterly.

FOUR WEEKS LATER

As the light faded that night, I found myself in a bizarre place, twisting with one dream after another. I don't want to disappoint anyone but I saw no light at the end of a tunnel. Micah's face continually faded in and out, ranging from his childhood to the present.

I will share with you now the most vivid of dreams and you can make of it what you will. I don't care to influence you with the occurrences that happened on the ill-fated night that I was shot. All I know without question is what I saw and the events that transpired.

I was standing in a valley of lush greenness and I saw God. There was a distinct figure on his right side and I knew it was Jesus. They were shrouded in a vapor that seemed to have a life all of its own. All your life you hear this stuff and then you are confronted with something so authentic. Don't get me wrong. I always believed, but I also doubted. What was it a man once said to Jesus? *Lord I believe, help me my unbelief.* That is probably true for most of us. At least the man was honest and I suspect that endeared him even more to the heart of Jesus.

Okay, back to the dream, vision, call it what you will. God was not the scowling figure I feared him to be. But he also was not going to embrace me. What I saw was sorrow etched upon his face that I had chosen the roads I had.

His expression reminded me of when Micah was little and he did something wrong and I knew I had to punish him but I did not care to. He sighed. Honestly, God sighed, and then he said how I wish you would have completely embraced my path. They turned to walk away.

"No!" I heard a sudden scream. They turned back and I don't blame you if you choose not to believe this but it is as I tell you.

My mother stood between God and me. "No, Lord. Not my only son. I have served you faithfully and I never once asked for anything for me specifically, but now I do and you must grant it."

My meek mom was almost belligerent with God. I waited for him to smite her. My harsh Southern Baptist upbringing still weighing heavily on me.

"Julie, he is gone."

Julie is not my mom's name. But then I recalled how

God sometimes changed the names of his servants. Even with my limited biblical knowledge, I know that Paul was once Saul. Somehow, I knew the meaning of the name Julie was youthful. My mom always reminded me of a little child when it came to her faith. So youthful just fits, don't you think?

"His time is up."

Mom stood defiantly, refusing to budge. "Remember Lazarus, Lord?"

God smiled. You would believe this if you knew the heart my mom has. She can melt anyone and not even God is immune to her tenderness, compassion, and grace.

"What makes you think he would turn even if I were to grant this request of yours?"

Mom said nothing but she stood there between God and me refusing to back away. Jesus placed his hand on his Father's shoulder. He whispered something that I could not hear.

It seemed several minutes passed by, but I am dreaming so I have no clue as to the length of time. Finally, God said softly. "It is as you ask my dear child. I will see you very soon."

They walked away and disappeared into the shroud of mist.

§

"Dad. Dad."

I could hear Micah's voice. I fought to open my

eyes. Finally, they were open but everything was blurry. The light hurt my eyes, and I motioned with a finger toward the source. Micah moved quickly and the room was dark—save the faint light that filtered through the blinds.

I felt his hands cup my face. "Welcome back, Dad. Welcome home." And then he began to sob and my little boy buried his head on my chest carefully avoiding the maze of tubes.

I died three times that night according to the doctors. The first time on Ellie's floor. The last time in the hospital when they gave up and a body bag was brought in. They placed my body into it and someone was zipping the bag shut. He had almost completed the task when my left eye blinked. I had no pulse for twenty minutes. I was gone. The medical staff tried to explain it to their satisfaction but to no avail.

I was in a coma for the next four weeks and there was still little hope that I would emerge. But here I am.

Now this next part that Micah explained to me makes me think of Forrest Gump saying, now you wouldn't believe me if I was to tell you. That is probably the case here but I kind of brought you along this far so it would be impertinent for me not to share the rest of this story.

The moment I died a very strange thing happened at the dementia facility where my mother resided. This same mother that did not recall that she was married or where she lived and struggled at times to even remember her children's names. It was just past midnight when Angel, one of the staff members, opened the door to mom's room. She discovered her kneeling by a chair and praying fervently. She recalled her saying, "No, God. Not my only son. You can't have him now. Send him back."

Angel called to her and mom turned to her and stated with conviction. "Leave me be. *This is my moment, where all my faith culminates as one.*"

The cloudy look was gone from mom's eyes, and Angel knew she was truly witnessing a miracle. They tell me that for the next two days mom rarely budged from that spot. She prayed without ceasing. She took very little nourishment.

My sister, Kate received two calls past midnight. The first one was from Jackson and soon after she received a call from Angel describing the events that were transpiring. Kate hurriedly dressed and drove in the darkness to witness this phenomenon.

She arrived a few minutes later and discovered mom kneeling beside the bed. She knelt beside her. Early the next morning, Micah's flight landed and Jackson picked him up at the airport.

Jackson had been the one to receive the first call from Bruce. Jackson called Micah and then he called my sister. Micah received a text from his Aunt Kate, explaining the miracle taking place at the dementia wing, while Jackson was driving him to the hospital. He demanded that Jackson drive him there. He told me later that he believed whatever was happening with mom was where the only hope was.

Jackson and Micah entered the room. Kate sat in a chair; head bowed praying. Mom was still on her knees praying. Micah knelt beside mom and put his arm around her. "Mimi," he called.

She turned to him. "Your dad is not leaving," she stated firmly, and then she returned to wrestle with God.

Later as we pieced this story together, we would discover that five minutes before midnight on what should have been my last night on this earth—Angel looked in on mom and she was sound asleep. Angel had no idea why she felt compelled to check on her again just minutes later.

As Micah knelt beside his Mimi that morning—that was according to the medical records the precise time that the body bag was almost zipped shut. So, in the end, what can we say about miracles, or is it more that mom wrestled God and won? What is the bigger story? This is my story and I will tell you that I do not possess the answers. It proved something I always thought to be true and that is that my mom held a very special place in the heart of God.

She died two days later while I lie in a coma. She had rallied to do her last work on this earth. Ironically, from the time she rose out of that bed to pray no one saw a hint of dementia, and she became quite indignant with my sister when she was asked questions that she previously had not known the answer to in years. Her memory was crystal clear.

As much as I would have loved to have seen her when I finally emerged from my deep sleep, I was happy that she was free.

I would see her again one day.

You have to have faith that after the events that transpired when I became a modern-day Lazarus that even a knucklehead like me knew I was given a second chance to walk a different path.

Be best not to squander the opportunity. Don't you think?

ABOUT THE AUTHOR

Billy Beasley resides in Carolina Beach, NC, with his beautiful wife Julie, and their Australian Cattle Dog, Teke, who graciously agreed to play the role of Josie in his third novel, *The Girl in the River*. He shares two simple beliefs with his favorite character in his first novel, *The River Hideaway*—Faith in God, and a conviction that 'Hearts have no color'.